THE LINK THAT COULD NOT BE BROKEN

Suzanne—
To our fearless leader at
616 — thank you for your
enthusiasm for my first book!
Chitra Shff

C. L. SHAFFER

To my grandparents, Chester, Verda, Leon, and Bea
for being witnesses of their faith.

CHAPTER 1

LATE SUMMER IN 2003

The new café on Main echoed the building's history—a general store with creaky wood floors, a copper ceiling, and two wide-eyed windows separated by a rusting screen door coated with chipping green paint that led out onto a shaded porch. These were the things the current owners had decided to keep. The items they had added—the suspended TV's, modern lighting, and a mural of a farmer with corduroy fields of corn ready for harvest—blended so well with the old that they felt as if they had always coexisted.

The cafe is nearly empty, apart from a mother busy negotiating with her child as if the years between them were irrelevant. The toddler spins around in her dainty white dress, squeezing a clear plastic bottle of greenish-blue liquid that is nearly ready to burst. Gavin can see her twenty years from now doing exactly the same thing at a local bar.

He drums a few notes on the table with his thumb. He stops, rotates his wrist, and glances at his watch. It is 4:46. Faulkner is late.

A professor at local Millerstown College, Faulkner Brickley had been a part of Gavin's life for as long as he could remember. When Gavin was still a boy, on Sunday afternoons, while Gavin's minister father visited the aging members of his congregation, a sort of ritual took place between the younger Gavin and the professor—a kind of forum on things not usually spoken of in polite conversation, namely that of religion.

But no matter what topic the two found themselves engrossed in or how far they may have ambled down a subject's avenue, the professor would inevitably find a way to steer the conversation back to one simple question: "Gavin, what did Mrs. Brickley teach you in Sunday school this morning?"

The question was often met with a shrug of the shoulders, followed by a disinterested, "I don't know," as if the boy enjoyed the game of keeping from the professor the knowledge that he coveted the most. Gavin would hem and haw a bit more until the suspense of keeping it from his friend became, even for him, simply too much to bear.

In possession of his answer at long last, the professor would predictably find that he had a better way of explaining the lesson. As if on cue, he would let out a sigh, get up from his chair, and close the oak sliding doors that separated the living room from the kitchen in the hopes of barring Mrs. Brickley from overhearing the improvements made to her lecture. Even then, Gavin knew that the professor was very wise.

These meetings between Gavin and the professor continued and matured in subject as Gavin journeyed through grade school, high school, and then on to college. It endured even as he juggled his graduate studies, ministry work at the college chapel, and a counseling internship. Uninterrupted, it persisted as he began to work as a counselor full time in the same year that his minister father passed away.

More than six years after Gavin began working and one year after the professor's wife passed away, the custom remained. Today, however, the 31 year old, Gavin Bahn, would put an end to the practice.

The mother and daughter, who had been sitting near the front, leave, taking with them one oblong greenish-blue stain. "Nine to fivers" and college students turn up for their last coffee fix of the day, and the café begins to take on the appearance of a crowded hot spot.

Professor Brickley arrives. He looks around, and when he finds Gavin, he puts his hand up and points at him in a sign of recognition. He tucks his polo shirt back into his tan chino pants, exhibiting his flat stomach. Unusual for a man his age, it made him appear more like a celebrated football coach than a professor of theology, but as he takes a seat, he caps his knees with his hands and lets out the groan of an old man. "These kids seem to get noisier with every passing year," he complains while grinning at Gavin as if the joke was partially intended for him. "'And that ye study to be quiet,' First Thessalonians four-eleven," The professor quotes aloud for the students to hear.

Some of the kids at the cash register, who apparently know the professor, cheer loudly. He turns back toward Gavin and laughs while pointing his thumb at them. "Those are some of my students who want to be ministers. May God have mercy on them and on their congregations." He says this slightly louder so that they will hear him. They cheer and toast him with their to-go cups of coffee.

"How are you?" the professor asks Gavin.

"Good," Gavin answers, lying as best he can.

"Good," Professor Brickley says, shifting his body around toward Gavin but continuing to watch over his shoulder the students trailing out the door.

"My job is going well," Gavin says nonchalantly. "I get a kick out of it. Sometimes it gets a little predictable, I suppose. You know, it's the usual complaints: My boss hates me because I really hate my boss, my father wanted me to be a doctor, but all I ever really wanted to be was a carpenter—that kind of thing. Despite the predictability of it all, I really do find messing with people's heads satisfying."

Gavin glances up to see what expression Professor Brickley has on his face, to see if he has impressed him with his ability to manage through a tiresome world, but the look on the professor's face does not show that he is impressed. In fact, he seems to be only half listening. Gavin's attitude becomes more serious. "Things are moving in the right direction. I'm glad, now more than ever, that I didn't follow in my father's footsteps."

Professor Brickley turns his head slightly more Gavin's way.

"I'm glad, because I don't believe any more," Gavin finishes.

"You don't believe what?" the professor asks.

Gavin now has his full attention. "I don't believe in God."

Professor Brickley seems to think on this for a moment. "You're just disappointed," he finally says as if he has figured something out that Gavin has yet to.

"No," Gavin says, more loudly and more forcefully than he had intended. Lowering his voice but continuing with the same edge, he ends, "He simply does not exist."

Moving his café chair out from the table, Professor Brickley uses his hand to lift himself up. His age is shown in how he performs this simple everyday task. He offers Gavin a look of displeasure but says nothing as he walks to the door.

Gavin sits there for a while. He drinks his coffee. He stares out the window. He realizes that he should have foreseen the professor's dramatic reaction.

Eventually, Gavin gets up and puts down a tip for the café owner's wife, Verda, who for the past half hour has been faithful in keeping his cup filled. He glances at her and feels a kind of kinship. Certainly, Professor Brickley would have said to that, "There you have it; there is your proof for the existence of God."

⋀

Outside, a breeze is blowing and there is the smell of rain. Gavin slows his pace as he walks toward home. He feels a sense of alarm for the approaching storm, but he also finds a kind of pleasure in its danger, knowing that lightning could strike him, but it probably won't.

He passes by Memorial Park. The Victorian-styled lamps that line the walkway glow as if it were the middle of the night. On one of the benches, a person is sitting just out of reach of the light. The figure rises and then accelerates toward Gavin. From the dimness of the park, it emerges. Shadows slide off the figure, rapidly constructing its identity.

Gavin stands his ground, but Professor Brickley does not stop. Gavin glances down the road, considering an escape, but it is too late. The professor is before him, his forehead pleated like a window blind.

He looks Gavin in the eye, then at the street, and then at Gavin again. "You don't believe in God because you no longer know how to live." The professor's zeal grows with each word. "The world stinks because you don't live in it. You hide from it. You blame God for this, but it is actually your own doing. Surely one of the ways to experience God is to live and that is what you have stopped doing."

The professor's anger strikes at Gavin, and he is mute.

"You think I have not seen this before? Well, I have, and I will say this: It is far better to feel despair than it is to be numb and apathetic because at least with sorrow you have compassion. No doubt, it is good to have a little detachment from this world, but you have completely detached from it."

Gavin's silence persists as Professor Brickley rotates and then advances down the street back toward the café. Gavin stands there for a moment. He feels embarrassed, as if some truth has been revealed. He decides to head home, hoping that the feeling of being exposed will fade.

As he comes to the fourth block, rain begins to fall as the wind picks up. He notices a young boy straddling a bike on the other side of the street trying to get some newspapers into a bag. The child's caring manner for the papers surprises Gavin, but this feeling soon disappears as Gavin must tent his head from the rain with the side of his jacket.

He marches on in this uncomfortable manner until he hears what sounds like a screeching of a crow followed by a loud thump and the crunch of metal hitting metal. He looks out into the street and sees a truck stopped at an unusual place in the road.

Gavin's eyes focus in on the street. Before his mind can catch up, he is running toward the newspaper boy. He sees blood on the child's shirt. His bike is a few yards away, twisted with its various parts scattered about. A gust of wind sends the newspapers, which the boy had once held in his hands, down the street without concern. Gavin's head pounds and a cold sensation streams through his body as he kneels down beside the boy.

A clerk comes out of one of the shops. "Oh no," she says seeming to realize what has happened. She puts her hand on Gavin's shoulder and, before running back to her store, tells him she'll call for an ambulance.

A couple comes toward the scene, and once they see what has occurred, they begin to direct the traffic around the accident. A teenager emerges from the truck. He slams his fist down on the hood of the vehicle. He takes a few steps in reverse.

"Son, you don't want to do that," the man from the couple instructs. He then places his hand on the teenager's back and leads him to a bench.

Gavin crawls closer to the injured boy. He remembers from a television show that he should not move him. He tells himself not to, even though the impulse to do so is overwhelming.

He leans in closer to tell the boy that he will be all right, hoping that maybe this will somehow comfort him, but then he hears the child saying something that at first Gavin does not catch. The boy smiles at Gavin and closes his eyes.

For a brief moment, Gavin feels ashamed for his lack of emotion, but then he assures himself that it was okay not to feel something for a child he did not know.

"He's dead," Gavin states to the woman still directing traffic. The man from the couple comes over to Gavin to help him move the boy off the street.

Gavin's knees begin to shake, and he is overcome with weakness. He moves toward the empty bench where the teen driver had been sitting. Looking around, Gavin finds the teenager standing away from the crowd.

"Are you okay?" The man from the couple questions Gavin.

He asks this with such sincerity that for an instant Gavin is tempted to say no. "Yes," Gavin tells him.

The ambulance arrives and then the police. The group gathers in a small grocer to get out of the rain. A cop asks Gavin several questions. Gavin tells him what little he saw. He inserts his opinion that the accident had been a case of the boy not seeing the driver and vice versa. The officer interrupts him with a comment about the tragedy of losing someone so young and then ends by telling Gavin to get in touch with the police if he recalls anything else.

⅄

Stepping into his living room, Gavin takes a seat in the large overstuffed chair that is next to the window. The rain has stopped, and he looks out at his side yard. The light from his neighbor's kitchen illuminates the brick path and the ferns, hostas and anemones that line it. His father, who had owned the house before him, had planted the garden, and for whatever reason, Gavin had not altered it.

Tired of the view, Gavin goes to the kitchen to make a sandwich. Slicing his creation in two, he scrapes his finger with the knife. "Dang," he says out loud. Examining his finger, he sees there is no wound. He reminds himself again of his low threshold for pain.

He returns to his chair and devours the sandwich without bothering to savor the taste. The day's events clutter his mind. He senses the numbness that Professor Brickley spoke about. It had been injured by the death of the boy, but it was already beginning to cure, despite the boy's last words that played again and again in his mind.

He thinks about the boy's family, especially the father, who by giving him a newspaper route had probably wanted to teach the kid discipline, hard work, or something else along those lines, not knowing that it would be the last lesson he would ever teach him.

The family's pain seems foreign to Gavin now, and for just a moment, he wishes he could replace his nothingness with their agony. He conceives that at this moment they probably would not mind exchanging their agony for his lack of feeling.

His neighbor's light goes out. Gavin finishes his last bite and heads for bed.

In the morning, he calls into work and asks his secretary to cancel his appointments for the next two days. She sounds surprised but obliges, knowing that it has been years since he's taken any time off. He goes through his morning routine but at a much slower pace. Half an hour later, he heads out the door toward Millerstown College.

Passing by the street of the previous night's incident, he finds no evidence that anything had taken place. The rain had washed it away. He glances at the gutter, expecting to see lumps of newspapers there, but they too have disappeared.

This section of town feels different to him. The boyhood memories of riding a bike up and down its streets are replaced with an anxious unfamiliarity. The street appears too real instead of blurry from memories. Uncomfortable, Gavin continues on.

Professor Brickley's class is already underway when Gavin enters through the back of the large lecture hall of Old Main. Gavin takes a seat in the last row.

Talented in lecturing, Professor Brickley was also gifted at directing an entertaining debate. He knew who to call on to get the thing going and who could lighten the mood and get everyone laughing when things got too heated. He understood the skeptics, the believers, and those who seemed to not care. He understood that they all had something to say—it was just a matter of when.

Gavin sits back and watches his friend at work.

"Mr. Emory," Professor Brickley says, pointing at a student wearing a baseball cap sitting in the front row, "you have been unusually quiet today."

"Yeah," Mr. Emory agrees, lifting his gaze from his notebook, "I was just trying to work out a response to Anderson's point."

"If you think you have it, please share."

"Okay, well you know how atheists say that they don't believe that there is a God? Well, I don't believe that there are atheists. They don't exist." A few chuckles come from the back of the class. Mr. Emory grins and continues, "Their behavior provides evidence of this. They protest against the believer, participate in debates with the believer, and write interpretations from findings in science to prove the believer wrong. They fight against the idea of God…which for them would be like watching a person fist fight with nothing but air." Mr. Emory pulls off his hat and scratches his head. "I mean, who is more ridiculous? Is it Larry, so and so, the atheist who fights against a God who he claims is not really there, or is it Bruce, the Christian who prays to a God who he believes is really there?"

Professor Brickley rubs at his chin. "Interesting, Mr. Emory, however, can anyone tell me where Mr. Emory went wrong in his argument?"

"Yeah," a kid in the back answers, "he claims atheists fight against something that they believe doesn't exist when he himself is fighting against atheists who he claims don't exist."

"Thank you, Mr. Townson, however, the real problem with Mr. Emory's argument is that atheists would actually say that they are not fighting against God but rather *for* their own truth."

Professor Brickley looks around the class. "Anyone have any suggestions on how to salvage Mr. Emory's argument?"

"My brain is too tired after that one," a kid sitting near the front row utters.

Professor Brickley glances at him. "You may rest when you leave my class, Mr. Cooper."

An older woman near the middle of the room raises her hand. "I think Emory could have kept the beginning of his statement and then gone into why he thinks atheists really do believe there is a God but that they are just mad at Him."

"And why would a person be mad at God?" Professor Brickley asks.

"I know of several reasons for this: lousy childhood, some tragedy that has befallen them, an inability to explain evil."

"Not to embarrass you, Mrs. Jamison," Professor Brickley states, "but I get the feeling that you have had some firsthand knowledge of this?"

"You would be correct in assuming that."

"And this brings me to my point, class. I permitted this debate to get a bit unbecoming. I tolerated some trickery in your arguments. I also allowed some of you to be a little condescending, even though you had no right to be in order to see if anyone would notice what was missing from your arguments. Is anyone able to tell me what was missing?"

The class goes silent for a moment, and a girl in sportswear with a ponytail raises her hand. "When I was listening, I wrote something down." She says and then glances at her note pad, "While we show off our heads, love lies here dead."

"Thank you, Miss Newman," Professor Brickley says. He then turns to the entire class. "The letter that Paul wrote to the church in Corinth tells us, 'charity never faileth.'" Professor Brickley states this with such strength and charge that it pulsates out into the class like the ringing of a gong. He picks up a pencil from the podium and holds it up for the class to see. Some of the students, who were beginning to gather together their belongings, pause. "As the verses continue, 'But whether there be prophecies, they shall fail; whether there be tongues, they shall cease; whether there be knowledge, it shall vanish away.'" Professor Brickley pulls a pencil sharpener from his satchel. He fastens it to the desk next to the podium and begins to rotate the handle, sharpening the pencil. "And finally, 'For we know in part, and we prophesy in part. But when that which is perfect is come, then that which is in part shall be done away. When I was a child, I spake as a child, I understood as a child, I thought as a child: but when I became a man, I put away childish things. For now we see through a glass darkly; but then face to face: now I know in part; but then shall I know even as also I am known. And now abideth faith, hope, charity, these three; but the greatest of these is charity.'" He points the sharpened pencil at the students, "first Corinthians, thirteen, eight through thirteen."

"Class," he says, putting the pencil behind his ear, "you will learn many things throughout your college career. Hopefully, your biblical knowledge will increase at least in my classes and that is a good thing, but for the believer, that is not the ultimate goal." Professor Brickley untwists the body of the sharpener, dumping the wood chips into his hand. "We must remember that '…these three remain: faith, hope and love. But the greatest of these is love.'" He blows on his hand, sending the pencil bits into the air. "Everything else will pass away." He sweeps his hand over the class. "Now get out of here before I exercise my right to give you a pop quiz."

Gavin remains and examines the scene. The more studious learners jot some notes down. Others just head for the door. The debaters of the class, like Anderson, begin to argue with one another over the professor's last remark. They do so, this time, with a bit more respect.

The purpose of all this debating, as Professor Brickley once had mentioned to Gavin, was to "encourage an internal conflict within the student body in order to get them to think more critically about their faith or lack thereof." Gavin figured that this internal discord would resolve itself quickly enough for most. Others would struggle with it for a day, a week, or for the rest of their lives.

He realizes that at some point this war must have occurred within him. Something had advanced silently, cutting off his defenses without his knowing until, at last, he found himself on its side.

As the next class begins to form, Gavin slips out the back. He spots Professor Brickley with a different group of students on the lawn outside. Approaching them, he overhears the professor's forceful tone breaking in over the steady chatter.

A male student, standing across from the professor, shakes his head in disagreement. "But you must also be good in this life to be accepted by God."

"Ah yes," Professor Brickley answers with a tone of frailness that was unusual for him, "it is easy to think this, especially when you are new to the faith when God is so close that it seems easy to follow the Law and do good, but as you grow and continue to try, you'll see. You'll discover that even though you may want to, you often don't get it quite right. Imagine a pie chart." Professor Brickley's words strike the air with renewed strength.

"More business analogies?" Matt complains.

"Yes, Mr. Selway, I spent twenty years of my life in the business world, so there will be many business analogies. Now, as I was saying, this pie chart represents how well you lived for God. It is possible, like the thief on the Cross, that someone might have 0%. You Miss Halsman," he says, turning to a pretty brunette next to him, "may have 85%, while Mr. Selway over there may only have 3%."

"Hey," Matt protests.

"The point is, Matthew, that none of us is or will ever be 100%, but God's grace through faith in Christ makes it so. That is the essence of the Good News."

The professor turns to the rest of the group. "Of course, there is another side to all of this," he says, folding his hands together. "If that thief on the Cross had been given the chance to live, then there would have been some evidence of his sincere commitment to God by the way in which he lived out the rest of his life." He points at the students, "if you have truly put your faith in God, the proof will be there in how you live. In other words, good works cannot bring about salvation. Rather, good works are simply evidence of that salvation."

Professor Brickley looks in Gavin's direction. "Now remember, next week I've altered our schedule a bit. Instead of covering 'God doesn't need your faith, but you do,' we'll be discussing whether or not a Christian is still saved after they lose their faith and if it is really true that your relationship with God is the link that cannot be broken." He moves from the circle of students and walks steadily toward Gavin, gaining speed as he nears him.

"I was enjoying your discussion," Gavin offers.

"I'm sure," Professor Brickley answers, passing Gavin by.

Gavin scrutinizes the area to see if anyone has noticed the snub, but then the professor motions with his hand. "Walk with me to my next class. I'm late."

Gavin points in the direction of the group. "Students of yours or just some kids you met along the way?"

"No, they're my students, Gavin." Professor Brickley stops abruptly. So much so that Gavin has to reverse his path and walk back to him. "One of the professors said that there was an accident in town yesterday. I didn't get all the names of who was involved, but your name did come up."

"I was only a witness to the accident," Gavin replies matter-of-factly.

"They said the boy died in front of you, Gavin!" Professor Brickley then mutters something to himself and seems to get snagged by a thought that, for a moment, appears to immobilizes him.

Impatient, Gavin disrupts the silence, "I actually came here to apologize for the way I sprang that bit of information on you last night."

Still distracted, Professor Brickley answers, "No, I should be the one to apologize. I should have responded more calmly. I talk to atheists all the time in the classroom, and half the time, they're the ones who are going to be the pastors, so I should be used to it. It's just that..." The professor stops and then continues, "I had hoped that it would not happen to you."

The professor glances at the ground and then shifts his gaze back to Gavin. "Would you mind coming to my office Saturday evening? I have something I want to share with you."

Gavin cringes a bit. "If you're thinking of having some kind of 'ye must not backslide' session, just count me out."

"I'll see you Saturday," the professor replies in a successfully detached manner and then commences his journey toward the classroom.

CHAPTER 2

Gavin takes a seat in front of a bowl of cereal. He had four other chairs at the table, but he never made a habit of sitting in any of them. He begins to wolf down his dinner, sending a cool stream of milk onto his chin. He wipes his mouth with a dishtowel. Quickly scooping up another large spoon full, he stops himself, realizing that there was no need to rush. He slows his pace and takes a deep breath.

After finishing, he goes to the sink. Turning on the faucet, he watches as the cereal flakes liquefy and disappear into the small holes of the drain. He punches off the water, hearing something at the front of the house. He notices it again and marches toward the door. At the end of his driveway, amongst his now overturned garbage cans, is a boy about 8 years old on a bike.

"What are you doing?" Gavin barks from the porch. Bags of black plastic, deformed by their contents, have rolled out of their cans and into the wet street. The thought of having to pick up the slimy bags only adds to Gavin's irritation.

"I'm sorry, sir," the boy utters softly.

Gavin takes his attention off the garbage and glances back at the child. He is terrified.

"What happened?" Gavin asks stepping from the porch.

"I didn't mean to run into your garbage. It was an accident." The boy begins to cry.

"Hey, okay. Are you hurt?"

The youngster shakes his head as he wipes his nose with the back of his hand.

"Why don't you just help me put these bags back in the cans, and we'll forget all about it."

The boy lays his bike down on the grass. As he tosses in the last bag, he stands there looking at Gavin. "You knew my brother," he finally says.

"I did?"

"He was the one who…died in the street."

"That was your brother?"

"Yes."

Gavin appreciated the child's straight forwardness, but he felt sucker punched. He needed to sit down. He directs the boy over to the porch steps.

"My aunt knew your father, the minister, and where he lived. I overheard her talking about it this morning when she read what the paper had said about the accident. I guess I figured if I found your father, I'd find you."

"My father passed away a number of years ago. I inherited his house," Gavin explains, wondering why he was telling his history to a child.

"Did…my brother say anything to you before he died?"

Gavin looks out at the street. "He did," Gavin answers and then prepares himself to tell the kid what he had every right to know, but then the boy gets up from the step and goes to his bike.

"Will you be at the funeral on Saturday?"

"Ah, no I don't think so," Gavin answers. "A funeral is more for a family and for people who were a part of your brother's life."

"Weren't you there when he died?"

"Yes."

"Then you were a part of his life." The child jumps on his bike. "The funeral is at 10:30 at the Evangelical Free Church on Pine."

"Yes, I know the place," Gavin replies as a bladed memory jabs at his mind.

The boy rides off, and Gavin immediately feels foolish for not asking his name. He walks back inside, exhausted as if just home from a long day at work. He heads toward his chair but then hears someone coughing out on the porch, followed by a knock at the door. He opens it and sees Professor Brickley standing with his back to him, looking out at the street. "Weren't we meeting on Saturday?" Gavin asks.

Professor Brickley turns. "I thought it important that we discuss this now."

"O…kay," Gavin says, heading to the kitchen with Professor Brickley trailing him.

The professor lets out a long sigh as he takes a seat at the table. He clears his throat, pulling some papers out of a leather satchel. After retrieving everything he wants, he leans on the table. "Every now and again, I wish I could hear my grandmother pray." He scratches the top of his head in a frustrated manner. "Her prayers were fiery, emotional utterances.

"During church services when she was asked to pray out loud, it was as if she would forget that others were around. It was as if it was just her and God. For me, at the age of 14, this was quite embarrassing. "The professor glances at Gavin. "We are often foolish when we are young."

Gavin shakes his head, knowing that the comment was intended for him.

Professor Brickley says quietly, "Now that I am older and life has gotten a bit harder, I would give anything to hear one of my grandmother's prayers." He stares at the top of the table for a moment.

"God has given us all gifts to either choose to use or not to use. To produce good or evil from them, I believe, is a choice He has given us. My grandmother was blessed with two talents, praying and cooking. Her prayers brought about much good. I am sure of that. Her cooking, on the other hand, produced many large stomachs that, to this day, some in her hometown are still trying to figure out how to get rid of. Research, I believe, is one of my talents. Some might say that teaching is another. During finals week, both are considered evil."

Gavin lets out a laugh, and Professor Brickley leans back in his chair, waiting for him to finish. He then stretches out his hand as if to literally try and grab Gavin's attention. "Now, let me tell you a true tale: I had a dream so curious that when I awoke, I wished I could have taped it so that none of the details would be lost. I saw a woman place a child at the base of a fortress. The fortress was solid and fortified. It taught the child many things. Then, without warning, the fortress fell. The child then came to sit under another fortress. This one was ancient with crumbling stones. What took place next, at the time, I could not remember. The last part of the dream I did recall, however.

"The child became a man, and I got the sense that he had been told some-thing important in the part of the dream that I could not recollect. Then I saw a name, possibly a name of a city. Then there was a sound, the sound of a woman's voice. The voice echoed and seemed to be everywhere. A minor point of the dream I thought at the time. The dream ended with the man carrying out a task.

"When I awoke, I just laid in my bed. The yearning to remember the part of the dream that I could not recall was so intense that I began to sweat as if I had broken a fever. The sweating soon was replaced by an overwhelming hunger. I had never felt such hunger before. I jumped out of my bed and made my way to the kitchen. I had to eat something, anything. As I got to the kitchen, I fell to my knees in awe as I recalled that missing part of the dream."

Professor Brickley glances down at something written on his papers. "As I said earlier, we can either choose to use our talents or not to use them."

Gavin shifts in his seat, feeling a little irritated by this switching back and forth of subject matter, but he decides to be patient, knowing how the professor enjoyed working an audience, even if it was an audience of one.

"I have to ask why you, Gavin…why have you chosen not to use your ability. Why have you chosen not to do the thing we both know you should be doing. You have seen the empty side of life. Why do you continue to live in it?"

Gavin stares at the table like a child being scolded. Professor Brickley had never said so, but Gavin had always guessed that the professor had been disap-pointed when Gavin had abandoned the ministry.

"Gavin, I would have given anything for you not to have gone down this path. You have thrown away all that you once felt passion for."

Out of curiosity or out of simple respect Gavin lifts his head and sees Professor Brickley's watery eyes.

"At the very least," the professor continues, "I would have expected you to find the extraordinary in the occupation that you are pursing now. Men can certainly find the remarkable in the things that they must do, but you don't even do that. You crack jokes about your work. Is nothing sacred?

"Of course, a man's worth is not found in what he does but in who he is. There is an intrinsic value to a human being no matter what he or she is, but character is vital. And it is a lack of character that will, no doubt, be the result of your present callousness.

"I am not sure what you will do with what I am about to tell you—what I am about to show you. It is a great discovery. I want to tell you about it because I am hoping that it will be the catalyst to killing your numbness. However, when everything is said and done, you'll need to find your own way out of the hole that you've dug for yourself.

"I had hoped that some good would have come out of that boy's death after I heard you had witnessed it—that it would have triggered something in you, but I can see that it has not. I so want you to see that life can be extraordinary, but I cannot talk you into believing this. You are going to have to come to that conclusion on your own. Now, do you want me to tell you this discovery?"

Gavin's frustration grows. "Why do you feel that it is your duty to help me?"

"Ah, Gavin, that is what you have forgotten. We are here to help each other," he proclaims with a slight dramatic flair. "This is your moment, Gavin. Next time, I won't ask." Professor Brickley pauses. "I thought I taught you better than this?"

"Maybe you taught me too well."

"What do you mean?" Professor Brickley asks uncharacteristically, as if he really did not know the answer.

"How do you think it influences the man when you teach him when he is still a boy everything there is to know about life? The wonder of it is taken from him. You taught me so much that I had no reason to go out and experience it."

"Knowing something is quite different from experiencing it, Gavin. But I concede to my responsibility in this. Knowledge can be a kind of hindrance, especially if you think you know everything or if you believe that what you know is the Truth and it is not." The professor clears his throat. "But Gavin, if you are truly standing before me, blaming me for your faith failing, then maybe it is even more appropriate for me to encourage you to do this, because what I have to tell you will change your world."

"I'm sorry, Professor Brickley." Gavin stands from the table. "With all due respect, I'm simply not interested."

Professor Brickley gathers his belongings, "I still want to see you on Saturday." Professor Brickley moves around him. "And Gavin, you will be interested."

⚔

The next day at work, Gavin watches as the woman he is counseling curls the straps of her pocketbook around her fingers. She is a successful business woman, has a husband and four kids. Gavin assumes that this is a new thing for her, having problems outside the realm of her own management.

"And on top of everything else," she complains, "I've been having this reoccurring dream that is beginning to intrude on my daily life. Can we talk about that?"

"Of course," Gavin answers, glancing at the clock.

The woman nods. "The dream starts with a figure moving across a field. I get the feeling that this person is trying to make her way to another place, because where she was before could no longer sustain her. She has trouble, however, moving to this new place."

"What do you mean?" Gavin straightens in his chair.

"Her movement is restricted. When the figure attempts to move to this other place, it always ends in injury. All I can see is this faceless body just lying there in the field."

"Who do you think the figure is?"

"I get the feeling that it is a friend of a friend. A woman…Nancy Hartman."

"Do you mean the mayor, Nancy Hartman?"

"Yes."

"How well do you know Nancy?"

"Not well at all. I've only met her once or twice."

"Do you feel a responsibility to Nancy?"

The woman hesitates as if she were contemplating a sociably acceptable response. "No, not really," she finally says. "However, I keep thinking that I need to tell her about the dream."

"Why?"

"In order…to stop something bad from happening to her."

"You believe the dream is a premonition?"

"I don't know. Maybe. Possibly."

"Who else do you think the woman might be?"

"I suppose it could be me, right? That's what you want me to say, isn't it?"

"No, but it's interesting that you would say that. Dreams are about what is happening in your own life. They do not predict the future, and neither do they provide secrets into other people's lives as you are suggesting. What is going on in your life? Are you being hindered from moving forward by some outside influence? Or are you the abstractionist, denying your own advancement, maybe in your career or in your personal life?"

The woman pauses, casting her gaze to the ceiling. "I have wanted to take some classes toward a MBA, but I just keep putting it off."

"Possibly tomorrow you should register for these classes."

"Shouldn't I say something to Nancy?"

"You could, but you said yourself that she is a friend of a friend. What influence do you really think you will have over her? Plus, in saying something, understand that it will not stop the dreams, because the dreams are about you, despite the fact that you want to make the mayor the main character."

"But the dreams are so powerful. They seem more important than something that is just about me."

"Never say you are unimportant. To your own mind, you are the most important one of all."

CHAPTER 3

It is Saturday morning. Gavin gets out of bed and picks out a dark suit from his closet. He looks at the clock. It is 9:10. He has almost an hour before he has to leave for the funeral. He is not sleepy enough to return to bed; his thoughts about the funeral have him fully alert.

He stumps down the stairs to the living room and sits himself down in the middle of the couch. Only on rare occasions did he ever sit in this spot and seeing his living room from this vantage point makes it appear strange, as if it were someone else's house.

On the coffee table, amongst a pile of old mail, he notices a book Professor Brickley had given to him. A layer of dust covers and surrounds it.

Years ago, when his faith was still with him, Gavin considered himself a devoted reader. He believed, at the time, that a book well chosen was something that was selected for you—as if God Himself had guided your hand amongst the thousands of other books on the shelf to the one you should read.

A book badly chosen, however, for reasons of an alluring cover or because it received a lot of publicity, was often, more than he would like to admit, abandoned. These would end up on various pieces of furniture throughout the house where they took on the same occupation as that of a wooden box or a statue of an animal.

Twenty minutes into reading the book that Professor Brickley had given to him, Gavin realizes why he had banished this one to the coffee table. He closes it, forgoing to mark his place where he had left off. He slides it back onto the table, bulldozing a line of dust onto the floor.

On the mound of stale mail, he notices a postcard. He picks it up and flips it over. The postcard is for the grand reopening of a local hotel that has been recently renovated. Beneath its typeset name in gold is a picture featuring its high ceilings and ornate crown molding. Straight lined modern tables and chairs furnish the establishment. A small menu at the very bottom lists its specialty: prime rib.

Gavin jabs the point of the card to his lip. Some evening he will keep his work suit on and check out the renovated Mosley Hotel.

At 10:10 a.m. He begins his walk to Pine Street. The day is bright and much warmer than what he had expected. Regret hits him for not going to the coffee-house before the funeral.

Turning onto Pine Street, he sees a large gathering of people on the church steps, dressed in varying shades of black and grey. The scene reminds him of a hundred other funerals that he had attended with his father.

As a preacher's son, he had always preferred a funeral to a wedding. He was much more comfortable in the reserved atmosphere of a funeral, but even as a boy, he realized that there were times when some funerals were more festive than some weddings.

He enters the church and moves in among the funeral attendees. He allows others to go before him, reminding himself that he is the least important person in attendance. He takes a seat in the second to last row. The smell of decaying hymnals, the familiarity of the hard pew, and the rustling conversations of people greeting each other eases him. He glances at the pulpit now, feeling much braver than when he first entered the church.

He had never been awestruck with his father's ability to preach. His father's skills were better suited for caring for people one on one. Nevertheless, his finest sermons were those that contained a lesson from his own life: a story about God's faithfulness, inspired from an incident of rushing a friend to the hospital; a sermon on learning from one's mistakes, taken from an attempt at French cuisine; or an account of a broken heart, aroused from the life of a pastor who had lost his wife when his son was only 3 years old.

"Gavin Bahn?" a woman in her 70s asks, extending her hand to greet him. She had a jovial smile, but her structured suit conflicts with this. She reminds Gavin of someone running for political office. "How are you?"

Gavin takes a moment to place her. "I'm fine. How are you, Mrs. Snyder?"

"Oh, I've got a few pains here and there, but it's nothing to complain about," she explains with a laugh, a laugh almost inappropriate for a funeral. "Oh, here comes one of my pains now," she continues with her unchecked cheerfulness. She motions to an older gentleman coming their way. The man rests his hand on the back of the pew, allowing it to support some of his weight.

"You remember Pastor Bahn's son, right Chester?" She curls her head down to look into the older man's eyes.

The older man thinks for a moment as if he were going through a lifetime of memories. "Ah, yes, of course, Gavin Bahn," he responds with a coarse voice followed by a cough. "Chester Snyder at your service." He slices his hand through the air, grasping Gavin's with unexpected strength. "I was in the choir."

"You were the one with the deep voice," Gavin answers, remembering.

"Yep, that was me, but the pipes don't work as well as they used to."

"It was good to see you, Gavin," Mrs. Snyder states, barely allowing her husband to finish.

"Yes."

"We better get a seat, Chester," she suggests to her husband anxiously. They hurry off but are stopped three or four times by couples and individuals who want to chat. They are the last couple to take a seat, and as Gavin remembers it, they always were the last to take a seat before the start of Sunday service.

There is no casket at the front of the church, only an urn surrounded by flowers and a collage of the boy's brief life. The idea that the child's body no longer exists, shocks Gavin for a moment. A thought drifts in and instructs him that the body is only a shell. Gavin shakes it off, reminding himself that the philosophies of his father would take time to rub out.

The organist begins to play a rendition of "The Lord's Prayer." A haunting version of the song, it seems to fill the church with a thick cloud of mangled recollections.

Gavin notices the young boy from yesterday coming out of the office door that is to the right of the pulpit. A woman of average height accompanies him. Her face is colorless, offset with eyes the color of a black marker.

Gavin can tell that the boy has been crying, but the woman appears calm, in charge of her emotions. She reminds Gavin of the many mothers that often come into his office who, alone in their daily cares of home life, feel that they must appear to remain steadfast, not just for their own sake, but for the sake of their children.

The woman places her hand on the boy's shoulder. For some reason, this causes Gavin's memory to snap back into place as if it had been unaligned with his present conscious mind. "Elizabeth?" He says, inserting his voice into the dreary silence.

An elderly woman sitting next to him turns her head his way and frowns as if Gavin had spoiled the atmosphere for her. He smiles at her and then returns his attention to the woman at the front of the church, but she has already taken a seat in the front row.

He roughly opens the bulletin that he had been given when he arrived. He reads a short passage, italicized in the middle of the inside page. He passes over words like "celebration" and phrases like "a joyous journey from this life to the next." He continues to scan down through the page and then sees the name Justin Connor and reads, "Surviving is his aunt, Elizabeth Kashner and older brother, Thomas Connor." He scolds himself for not getting a newspaper. He could have avoided all of this. "Dang it," he whispers, and the woman next to him nudges him with her elbow.

It had been outside a convention center on a cold blistery day that Gavin had first met Elizabeth Kashner. A well-known apologist had been invited to speak, and the tickets were on a first come, first serve basis. Noticing her in line behind him, he had turned around and joked, "You know, I'm going to be the last one to get in."

She had answered back, rubbing her ears that were red from the cold, "Sir, I do believe you have miscounted."

When to both of their amazement this actually did occur, he immediately asked her if she was a Christian. When she told him that she was not, he handed her the last ticket and wished her a good night.

Later at a coffee shop nearby, they met again. He outstretched his hand, "Bahn, Gavin Bahn," he had said, making her laugh.

She then invited him to join her. She inquired as to why he was there, and he told her that his ride was only able to pick him up after the event. Not wanting to make her feel bad about accepting his ticket, he changed the subject and asked her how she had liked the service.

"I liked it very much," she said with what seemed like the first real smile she had had in a very long time.

"I see," he said. "That's wonderful."

"Yes."

"In fact, I think that's just about the best thing I've heard in some time," he had continued. And as they walked to the door and conversed for another few minutes, with neither of them wanting to leave, but Gavin pointing out that his ride was waiting, he ended the conversation by inviting her to church.

After that first meeting, their friendship had grown, and so too did her faith, a faith that would eventually spread to the rest of her family.

But then there was the day with an open grave—a day colored in grayscale. Gavin had looked at her with such grief. Grief, that at the time, she must have thought had only been for the passing of his father, but then he had uttered to her, "I want you out of my life."

Gavin folds the bulletin in half. It seemed to him that the pivotal moments of his life always took place after someone had been buried. He runs his finger across the edge of the fold. He was determined to make sure that this funeral did not continue the pattern.

A short prayer is said, and Elizabeth turns to the congregation, "Thank you all for coming. We are having a gathering at our house. You are all welcome to join us."

The congregation rises from their pews. Some head straight for the door, while others begin to gather in small groups. Gavin stands and waits for Elizabeth to exit through the office door. He makes his way to the front, moving between the sets of people.

The funeral had been a collection of testimonies about Justin's life. Sunday school teachers, Scout leaders, and grandparents had stood and told their tales about the youngster. Gavin had assembled a picture of Justin. He had loved to fish with his grandfather. He had once danced the tango to the B-I-B-L-E song in Sunday school. When asked who the sons of Noah were he had answered, "Shem, Ham, and tuna fish." Gavin would have liked him.

Moving through the groups of people, Gavin overhears conversations about the accident, about how it took place and other personal information about the family. "First Thomas loses his parents in a car accident and now this. It's just too much for a child to bear," one woman says quietly to another.

"Certainly is," replies the other.

Upon reaching the picture collage, Gavin studies each snapshot carefully, more so than the other people who have just casually passed by. In most of the photographs, Justin has his arm around a family member or a friend, supplying a humorous facial expression. In a few, he is alone, appearing as if he is unaware that the camera is in front of him, his attention on a coloring book or a toy.

"Mr. Bahn?" Thomas Connor says, moving out from a circle of people, his cheeks flushed from the heat of being surrounded by the crowd.

"Yes," Gavin responds, greeting him with a handshake.

"My aunt told me your name after I got home the other night," he says, smiling with red eyes. "She then sent me to my room."

"Oh?"

"Yeah, I wasn't supposed to be riding my bike by myself." He points to the collage. "My brother was a bit of a cutup. He was always making a goofy face. Grandma would complain that you couldn't take a serious picture of him. If you wanted one, you had to do it without him knowing." Thomas stops and swallows hard. "Are you coming back to the house?"

"No."

"But you have to. It's all been set up. You are going to drive with me and my grandparents."

Gavin pauses for a moment and then directs the boy to an isolated section of pews, a section that Gavin and his friends once referred to as the "seats of merriment." The label was short lived; however, for after two Sundays of excessive laughing, goggling at the opposite sex, and one moment of audible flatulence, Gavin had been moved to a seat—dead center—front row.

Remembering, Gavin pats the arm rests. His mood then turns serious, "Thomas, ah, your aunt and I used to be friends. I haven't seen her in a very long time, and I don't think that this is the appropriate time to get reacquainted."

"So you were old friends?" Thomas asks, his legs dangling from the chair. "Yes."

"So what's wrong with seeing an old friend?"

Gavin laughs, hangs his head, and decides to give up.

"Come on; let's go outside," Thomas says. "My grandparents will meet us there."

Gavin kicks a few stones off the landing of the front steps, waiting for Thomas' grandparents, Bea and Leon, to show up. Thomas climbs onto the metal railing and stares out at the street. "It's tough imagining that you will live forever, isn't it? It's like your brain can't make it out."

"I guess if you believe in that."

"What? You don't believe that?"

"No."

"Wow. So you think you'll just stop existing?" he asks, wiping his nose with the back of his hand.

"Yes."

"Real…ly? I've never met anyone who believed that." He pauses. "Don't you think that's sort of creepy? I mean that you'll just stop…being."

"Creepy? No." The answer seems to quiet the youngster for a moment, and he appears unsure as to how to proceed. Gavin looks away but feels Thomas still observing him.

"You're worried about seeing my aunt, aren't you?" the boy asks.

"No," Gavin replies defensively. He then exhales and softens his tone. "I'm just wondering what I am going to say to her."

Seeing his grandparents, Thomas jumps from the railing and then turns to Gavin. "You're going to tell her what my brother said before he died."

"Oh." Gavin says with a tight throat.

The grandparents have a new sports car, the color red. Thomas and Gavin squeeze into the back seat. The warm weather of the autumn day, once appreciated, is now a nuisance in the tight quarters encircled by hot black fabric. Gavin burns his hand on the sun-heated belt buckle. Thomas does the same, and they laugh at each other. The grandparents apologize for what they obviously cannot control, and they blast the air conditioning on high.

Gavin would have preferred a conversation about the new car, but the funeral had made the family, particularly Leon, much more introspective than Gavin remembered him being.

"Do you recall," Leon begins again, "the time I took Elizabeth target shooting, and she nearly shot her foot off? All because of that bug climbing up her leg."

Thomas puts his hand over his mouth and giggles.

"The guys at the VFW still laugh about that one."

Bea ticks her tongue as her husband lets out a laugh. "You know, Gavin," she says over Leon's amusement, "that we left the Evangelical Free Church after your father's retirement, but what you probably didn't know was that we came back when Elizabeth became their Director of Education."

"I've always regretted how our two families lost touch after your father's death." Leon inserts, his mood turning serious again.

"Yes, we always thought that you and—" Bea cuts her statement short, causing Thomas to peer up at Gavin with an inquisitive look.

"We're just glad to see you again, Gavin," Leon interjects. "It's been five years hasn't it? I suppose the last time you saw Thomas he was merely a toddler." Leon smiles at Thomas through the rearview mirror.

"It's been over six, actually," Gavin corrects.

Leon nods in agreement. "Elizabeth has done a great job helping us with her sister's boys."

Thomas' attention remains focused on the floor mat, and Gavin begins to feel pity for him for never having known his mother, but possibly Thomas would, like Gavin had, come to see that it was far better to lose one's mother without knowing her.

Before the air in the car can cool, they arrive at their destination. Gavin forces himself through the opening that has been created by the inclined front seat. He feels like a man being birthed from the hot entrails of a car. He avoids getting tangled by the seat belt but still stumbles out onto the road. Thomas just stares at him, and his grandparents apologize once again.

The cottage-sized house is situated on the outskirts of town. It is too small for all of the funeral goers. Congregated on the front porch are those that could not fit inside. Gavin examines the porch in concern and tries to figure out how he could get lost in the crowd. He glances at Thomas and immediately abandons the idea. Thomas would smoke him out with ease.

As they walk toward the porch, Gavin notices the loosened ties, omitted suit jackets, and cigarettes clinched between fingers. The breeze that is now blowing makes it apparent that the shirt under his jacket is sweated through. He flaps his jacket open and closed several times to cool himself.

"We're a pretty casual group. Feel free to take your jacket off," Leon explains, seeming to understand Gavin's discomfort. *Never take your jacket off at a funeral,* Gavin's father would always say. He decides to keep it on.

The group walks the long drive lined with overgrown lilacs. Leon avoids the crowd on the porch and leads the way to a side door. Bea enters the kitchen first, but Gavin can barely make it through the door. The room is jam-packed with people. Thomas excuses himself and shoves his way through the legs of adults that quickly reestablish their positions as he squeezes by. He reaches his aunt who is imprisoned between the stove and two other women.

At a safe distance, Gavin takes the opportunity to view Elizabeth more closely. Her hair is still brunette but longer now. Her face shows no evidence of the six years that have passed, but her figure is fuller, more womanlike. The warm comfortable feeling that he had for her all those years before returns. This time, it is punctuated with unexpected desire. He turns away to cause the emotion to dissipate. It was a funeral after all. When he looks up once more, he finds her strolling back into the darkness of the hallway.

He makes his way through the crowd and follows her path until he finds her alone in a bedroom. She is looking out a window, focused on something in the yard. She then turns slightly, possibly seeing his reflection in the glass. "Why did it have to be you?"

The words injure Gavin for only a moment. He rubs his forehead, feeling a slight headache coming on. "Thomas wanted me to tell you something. I don't think he'll leave me alone until I do." On the desk to his left, Gavin notices a small toy soldier. The soldier's arms and legs have been bent into the fetal position, making the doll appear as if it were in some kind of pain. In such a tidy room, the toy seemed out of place as if his platoon had abandoned him and headed for the safety of the toy box.

"I'm sorry he bothered you," Elizabeth offers.

"Don't worry about it," Gavin answers, feeling as if he were being dismissed. He did not like the notion, however, of her wanting him to go. He picks up the soldier, recollecting a memory from their shared past. He chuckles slightly. "Do you remember that Sunday School class we taught together?"

"Of course," Elizabeth responds faintly.

"I guess I was a bit of a control freak."

"The kids were terrified of you." Elizabeth answers matter-of-factly.

"Well, you have to admit, I had them acting like little soldiers, saying 'yes, ma'am', 'yes, sir', and standing at attention every time I came into the room."

Elizabeth turns more to him. "Except Calvin Drover." She smiles slightly. "He put an end to your regime, launching that cheese cracker straight at you."

"Yeah, and I made the mistake of throwing that cookie right back; it took us hours to clean up all those things."

Elizabeth lets out a laugh.

Gavin looks down at the toy. "At the end, your nephew believed he was going to a better place." Gavin utters as he straightens out the arms and legs of the figurine. "That should bring you some kind of comfort."

"You say that as if you don't believe it yourself."

"I don't." Gavin tosses the toy to the desk.

Elizabeth turns completely around. "I had hoped you were happy, Gavin. Maybe at times I wished you weren't…too happy, but I never wished for that."

Gavin glances at the toy. He wished it were still in his hands. He could use a diversion.

"I suppose you'd call all of this a coincidence," she says with a slight tone of annoyance.

Gavin waits for her to respond further, but she does not say another word. Her time for him was up. She had other things to do like mourn for her nephew.

He goes to leave, deciding to keep to himself the rest of what Justin had said to him. He closes the door, walks down the hall, and out the house.

⋏

The death of his father had seemed unjust to Gavin. He had died of injuries from a plane crash on his way to South America. That had been his father's idea of retirement, going to some unkempt corner of the world. Gavin had asked him not to go. He had told him to start acting like other retirees and put in some leisure time. His father had told him to shut up.

The accident had not even taken place over South America or even over another state, but the crash had occurred as his plane had taken off at the local airport. He and one other person were the only survivors.

When Gavin had arrived at the hospital, he was told that it was unlikely that his father would survive. At that moment, a strange emotion had come over Gavin. He had this overwhelming need to walk—to walk across town, across the state, and into the next; it did not matter where. Somehow, he thought that if he just kept moving, the collapsing feeling, that was taking place in his gut, would go away.

As he sat in the waiting room, he watched couples with children injured from rough housing or from playing baseball or football. He saw a man and wife pass by smiling, their arms around each other. These people were going through something very different from what Gavin was experiencing. They were walking out of the emergency room, relieved by how things had turned out.

At the time, Gavin wondered what frightened him more, the pain that his father was enduring or the grief Gavin would have to live with if his father didn't make it. He felt selfish for thinking such thoughts, so he held them back, telling himself that in a week or two he would be walking out of the hospital like the other people in the emergency room were, with his arm around his father. In just a short time, things would be as they always had been, and his father, the man he had always looked up to, would carry on as he always had.

Ever present, leaning against this hope, was the feeling that he was completely defenseless, as if all the control he had collected during his lifetime, from childhood to adulthood, had been handed over to some outside source. He had begun to pray at this reflection, remembering that he was not the one in control, but surprisingly, this only stirred anger. He wanted to be in control of the outcome. He didn't want God to have the power to move the pieces off the board, while allowing others to remain. Sitting in that waiting room, he could not make peace with this, and when the doctors finally came to tell Gavin the horrific news, he had already succumbed to his anger and grief.

Letting go of his faith, however, was not something that he had instantly decided. If he had, he would have most likely thought himself weak for losing his creed so easily, rendering some motivation on his part to maintain it. Instead, the opposite had taken place. The slow burning of his religion hadn't even taken his notice.

The prayer in the emergency room that had conjured up such anger was the last prayer he ever uttered. Looking back, he could see that it was this anger that caused him to forget that he could have turned to God for help. Instead, he took on the idea that thinking on God, on love, on hatred, on anything of any meaning, or intensity was a source of misery.

He began to tell himself to just keep going, living, and working. He told himself that he would be happier if he did this. He had allowed this motto to infiltrate his life so deeply that his faith soon became an unconscious habit, void of any extreme passions, and because of this, one day, his faith lost all meaning for him.

CHAPTER 4

It is evening. All the lights, except those in the hallway are turned off in the steel, modern building situated across from Professor Brickley's campus office. Three bands of light shine on the neatly trimmed lawn that separates the two buildings. The effect seems to be purposeful, as if it were someone's idea of a nighttime garden. The collective feeling of loneliness and contentment saturates Professor Brickley. He wishes for company but is glad for a peaceful moment to gather his thoughts.

He imagines his wife sitting with him as she occasionally would while he finished grading papers. Content to read a book while she waited, he would often interrupt her and read out loud a well-written paragraph with an interesting connection made by one of his students. With the commotion of both their days behind them, he could be alone with her and, at the same time, feel as if the entire universe were watching over them. That was how she made him feel: full, as if he were the center of everything. On rare occasions, even now, this feeling resonated with him as if she had never gone, and he was thankful for this, knowing that he was the type of person who always needed an audience.

He once had held the view that he should not marry her, thinking that if he lost her, it would be even more difficult to be alone. In the end, this notion turned out to be true, but he still hoped to come to accept that 'love' was a kind of self-restoring entity. Like an accident-prone starfish, he hoped that one day it would be able to repair the wounds it had caused.

But he lived in the present, of course. A present that at times seemed to span without end. The time in between was the most difficult—when there were no classes to attend or no visiting friends, when all there was to think about was the loss. During these times, it felt as if someone had closed a door, locking him inside. He knew she would be disappointed in how he was behaving now. If she were still alive, she would send him to bed without pie.

The telephone rings, drawing him from his thoughts. "I'm on my way. I'm just outside parking the car," Gavin says on the other end. Putting down the receiver, Professor Brickley picks up the bottle cap from his desk. Twirling it around in his hand, he glances up at the sword that was displayed in a glass case lined in velvet. Gavin's father had gotten him the sword, explaining that as a professor, many times, he would have to "cut through the bull."

Professor Brickley understood the meaning. He saw it in many of his students, the chasing after a philosophy or a radical idea simply because it was something new and exciting for the student.

"Professor Brickley." Gavin says with a tired voice, standing in the doorway observing the professor looking at the sword.

"Gavin, yes, come in," the professor says with his usual exuberance. He throws the bottle cap into the drawer and points to the wall. "The blade your father gave me."

"Yeah, I remember."

Professor Brickley pushes himself out of his chair. Rubbing his knee, he moves toward the sword. Upon reaching it, he opens the glass case and lifts the sword up and out of its rack. "A Civil War sword, your father told me. I was never interested in such things, but he was." Professor Brickley slides the sword out of its scabbard.

"He always enjoyed a good war story. Liked the strategy involved," Gavin explains, taking a seat in one of the chairs in front of Professor Brickley's desk.

"I think, more than that, he liked seeing good overcome an evil philosophy." Professor Brickley pauses and examines the sword more closely. "Do you remember the dream I told you about the other night?"

"Yes."

"The dream was about my demise."

"O…kay," Gavin responds.

Professor Brickley turns and glares at Gavin. He places the sword and scabbard in front of him on the desk. "Like giving an ancient Egyptian a cell phone—" he slaps both his hands down and leans toward Gavin "—is like giving prophecy to an unbelieving people."

Gavin looks away and groans.

"As I was saying, the dream was about my death. The second fortress was me; the first fortress was your father. The first fortress got cut down, but what I did not tell you was that at the end of the dream, the second fortress dies from a disease that spreads through its walls."

Gavin wipes his hand across his face, tired from the day's events. He sits up in his chair and gets ready for an argument. "I apologize again, Professor Brickley, but are you saying that you know how you are going to die?"

Professor Brickley ignores the question. "Let me tell you about a time when you were five years old." The professor begins to pace the floor. He taps the points of his fingers together, forming a triangle with his hands. "Mrs. Brickley was making you some spaghetti on the stove. You loved the stuff. I suppose most kids do. She was preparing the water and had gotten it to a real nice boil when she heard the sound of the pot falling and water splashing. She turned around and saw you standing with the spaghetti box in your hand, soaked with steam coming off your body. Later you had said that you were trying to help Mrs. Brickley cook."

"That's strange. I don't remember that," Gavin states with interest.

"I suppose you wouldn't have." Professor Brickley halts his pacing behind his desk. "Gavin, your life is about to change. I had always wanted you to go through this alteration in a manner that was less abrupt. But I can no longer be subtle. I feel my time is running out." Professor Brickley picks the sword off his desk. He turns it in his hands until it is perpendicular with his body.

"Are we getting into another discussion about my vocational choices? Because if we are, I—"

The sword slices diagonally through the air, cutting through Gavin's flesh from shoulder to shoulder. Gavin jerks back and gasps. He clutches at his ripped chest. For a moment, he compares it to the injury of his grazed finger that had occurred days ago. Or had that been weeks ago?

Confusion mixes with fear and he is frightened to view the gash directly. He slowly moves his hand from his chest and stares at his palm. He sees that the substance on it matches the same red substance that is all over the desk.

Unable to bear neither the pain nor the curiosity any longer, he looks down at his bloodied split shirt to the wound beneath it. "I thought I had on a white shirt?" he asks as his head falls slowly forward until it is stopped by the desk in front of him.

Professor Brickley snarls, taking on the appearance of a mad man. He backs up, gripping the sword as if he expects some kind of retaliation as Gavin's head begins to slowly rise off the desk.

Gavin moans loudly. Gaining awareness, he looks down at his chest. The wound that had been there only a moment ago is no longer upon his flesh. He turns his attention to his bloodied hand. "What did you do?" he utters as he attempts to get to his feet. With sword still in hand, the professor takes a step closer. Gavin grabs a coffee mug of pencils off the desk and throws it at the professor. He scrambles toward the door, but the chair leg gets in the way, and he trips into the corner of the room. "What have you done?" Gavin shouts.

Dropping the sword this time, Professor Brickley goes to him.

Gavin moves his arm into a defensive position. "Don't...come near me," he demands.

But the professor brushes aside the weak defense and puts his arms around him. "Gavin, my boy, I'm sorry. I had to do it."

"Why?" Gavin asks, regaining some composure.

Professor Brickley utters quietly in Gavin's ear, "this is your gift."

"I don't understand." Gavin says, slowly rising with the aid of the wall behind him.

"You should have been burned, Gavin, when the boiling water fell on you, but there were no scars on your face or arms. Emily later confided in me that she had seen burns on your arms, but when I came in from outside—when she had yelled for me—I did not see any. Your father said it was a miracle, and he took it as such without question. But I felt that there was something more to it, because there were other less dramatic occurrences too. You never were a very active or adventurous child so that is why you probably never noticed it, but Gavin, you are protected. Like Shadrach, Meshach, and Abednego when they found them-selves in the fire."

"That's just an allegory, Professor Brickley," Gavin snaps and then laughs at the professor.

"Some people believe that; I don't," Professor Brickley states defiantly, whipping his finger through the air.

"Apparently," Gavin counters, rubbing his chest.

A long silence falls between the two men. Gavin's disbelief bends, twists, and tries to adjust. He attempts to arrive at some logical conclusion to what he has just experienced. Possibly, it was a parlor trick or some kind of anomaly. He was not sure. His mind was having trouble just focusing in on the simple reality of Professor Brickley standing before him. Somehow he would have to find a way to prove to himself that this was all real. And then he would have to find a way to destroy the wonder of it.

Professor Brickley begins again, ending the silence. "The dream I had was not only about my death; it was also about you. The dream replayed the incident in the kitchen, but this time it provided an explanation for why you were un-harmed. Gavin, your purpose is to be unhindered. Do you understand what you could do with that gift?"

"What? You mean be like my father? This is all just too much, even for you. Why would I be given such a gift?"

"I don't know, but you must think about what good you could do with it."

"You're loving this, aren't you? But aren't you forgetting something? I don't believe anymore."

"A small matter that's not out of God's hands," Professor Brickley says matter-of-factly.

⋏

The conversation had ended abruptly, but Professor Brickley had achieved at least one thing. With one strike of a sword he had shaken Gavin's numbness and brought back all of his fears and emotions. Gavin understood at that moment what only a few knew: In the face of death, life is more real, more tactile.

There were probably a thousand different ways to die. He was not sure how many it would take to reinstate his numbness or to prove to himself that this "gift", as the professor referred to it, was real. He had only experienced two of them so far: the civil war reenactment that had taken place in the professor's office the night before and tonight's single misstep down a flight of stairs.

The second attempt had started out purposefully, but it did not end that way. He had stared at the marble stairs for over an hour, sipping at a cup of coffee, considering how it would feel and what it would make him into if he survived such a fall. It was a strange choice for someone who suffered from a fear of heights, but he figured it was much better than jumping off the roof. In the end, he had decided against the test, and turned away in order to toss his cup of coffee in the garbage can behind him. But he turned too close to the step's edge. Flapping his arms like a duck, he had fallen backward, headfirst down the stairs.

As he brushes himself off at the bottom of the staircase, slightly embarrassed by what had happened but obviously pleased with the results of having survived his headlong plummet down the spiral of marble steps, wall, and metal railing, his doubt still lingered. He wonders if he had the courage to do something else, something purposefully. Perhaps in doing something on purpose, not by happenstance, the doubt would be driven away. He then hears, in the distance, the whistle of a train. He could waste his time with a bunch of small trials or he could get right to it. The eerie whistle of the train sounds again, and Gavin decides that tomorrow will be his ultimate test.

Taking a seat on a bench, he places a bottle of chocolate milk on the cement pavement in front of him. The milk was a local brand that he had always found comforting. He could have chosen a more manly drink, but he needed to be fully alert for what he was about to do, and the comfort—which the milk, laced with chocolate provided—was what he needed now. He unbuttons his jacket, preparing himself for the test and the act that would surely serve to deaden his astonishment and make his "gift" commonplace because functioning properly with the wonderment of it simply would not do. There was only one way to do this—make it routine—by doing something extreme, something outrageous to convince himself that it was no big deal.

Hearing the train in the distance, he gets up from the bench, picks up the bottle in front of him, and walks to the outside track. A man inside the train station begins to yell at him.

The smell of oil and damp grass fills in around him. His mind seems to be having trouble dealing with two conflicting notions of wanting to live and the sight of a train bearing down on him. It nearly takes all of his might to just remain steadfast with his feet planted on the tracks and to ignore the natural instinct to step out of the machine's path. To quiet the commands yelling in his head, he takes a long drink from the bottle with his unsteady hand.

The increasing noise of metal on metal, the rhythm of the train's internal systems combine and pierce Gavin's ears. The lights of the train blaze at him and become more and more intense. His eyes ache. The claim that he tells himself, that this might be the most painful part of the process, is unconvincing. He drops the bottle, lowers his head, and takes two steps off the tracks. Losing his balance, he rolls down a slight incline of mud and wet grass.

The train sends up a gust of wind that twirls around him. Spitting into the grass, he laughs and shakes his head, "I guess I'm not quite ready for that." With the taste of oil thick in his mouth, he looks up and watches as the engine comes to a screeching stop. He gets to his feet and runs to a patch of woods. At the tree line, he turns to see a flashlight beam scanning the grassy knoll where he had come to rest.

Chapter 5

Shirtless, Thomas charges into the kitchen. His untied shoes flop off and on as he hurries across the tiled floor. "I need my blue shirt!" He shouts but receives no response. "I...NEED...MY...BLUE...SHIRT!"

"Okay!" Elizabeth replies, tossing a sandwich into a brown paper bag. "Turn your temperature to chill." She points to the door knob of the pantry door where a small blue shirt hangs. "Fresh off the press."

Thomas rolls his eyes and carefully takes the shirt from the hanger.

"Now Thomas, I want to ask you something."

"What?"

"You sent Pastor Kyle another email didn't you?"

"Maybe," he answers tying his shoes.

"Thomas."

"Yessss, but I had to. He was getting dogmatic about his own conjecture."

"Dogmatic? Conjecture?"

"Yeah, it means—"

"I know what it means, Thomas. I just didn't think...never mind. Anyway, you know what I told you about doing that. If you disagree with the pastor's sermons, you're to come and talk to me or grandma or grandpa. This is the last time I'm telling you this. If you don't stop emailing him—" Elizabeth combs her hand through her hair. "I can't believe I am saying this, but you'll be kept home from the Kid's Prayer and Praise services."

"You wouldn't."

"I would."

"You are a godless woman, Aunt Elizabeth."

Elizabeth frowns and flings the lunch bag at him. He puts it in his mouth, giggling as he finishes with his shoes. Elizabeth hurries to the couch, beginning to gather her belongings for the day.

"What are you doing?" Thomas mumbles with the bag still in his mouth.

"It's your first day back to school after..." She stops herself. "I'm walking you to school."

"What?" The lunch bag falls to the floor.

"I want to make sure you're safe."

"What? I don't need you to walk me to school!"

"You're not walking alone."

"I'm not alone. I'm never alone. I'm with six other kids and two sets of grandparents, one of which babysits me!" Thomas snatches up his lunch bag from the floor and storms to the door. "You're babying me again!"

Elizabeth stops in the middle of the room. She should have seen this coming; the experience of losing a brother had made Thomas, even more than before, want to grow up. "I love you, Thomas," Elizabeth answers, returning her pocketbook to the couch.

Thomas runs back and hugs his aunt tightly. "I like you," he states after a moment of consideration.

"That's fair."

Thomas races to the door and throws it open, banging it up against the interior wall.

"Thomas!"

"Sorry," he replies and runs out the door.

Down the porch steps to the sidewalk he races. He is far too preoccupied with greeting the other kids gathered in front of his house to notice the teenager passing by. The individual also does not seem to notice Thomas. His view is on the house. He takes a couple of steps toward the porch, turns, and walks back down the street.

⋏

Bland music plays as halogen lights do their best to light the space. They fail, allowing the dismal atmosphere to remain. The local farmer's market was a more charming place to shop, but today Elizabeth needed everything and needed everything fast, and the brand new superstore held everything within its gray cement walls.

Turning down aisle six, Elizabeth scans her mother's grocery list. They were the ninth item down: cheese puffs. She disliked the things. Oh, they were tasty little things, but the orange prints left behind by little fingers had always been a bit of an irritant to her. But the family, especially Justin, loved the snack.

She had forgotten that. It was strange how those little inconsequential memories kept fluttering back. Like how Justin would eat a handful every day with his two slices of apple and a grilled cheese sandwich.

She drops a bag into the upper portion of her cart. Tearing the sack open, she tastes just one, wanting the memory to linger. She takes another and then another, remembering bright sunny lunches full of silly conversations.

Feeling as if someone were watching her, she glances down the aisle, spotting a young man lurking near the potato chips. She looks down at her orange hands. *Great.* Embarrassed, she opens a roll of towels and rubs away the evidence. Tossing the open roll at the cart, it bounces off the edge, landing on the floor. The scroll unravels until it hits the bottom of the shelves and then spins back toward the cart. She sighs. *Terrific.*

⋏

Gavin would have gone to the small family grocer in town, but ever since the accident, he had kept away from the place. Besides, he had gotten accustomed to the efficiency of the brand new store on the outskirts of town. In fact, he was beginning to prefer it to the in-town grocer, where he had to make small talk with the owner.

Aisle seven quickly provides what he needs. He turns and hurries up the row toward the self-checkouts. On the way, he cannot help but eavesdrop on a conversation coming from the adjacent aisle. In fact, he tells himself that he has a legitimate reason in doing so since the woman's voice sounds familiar. He pauses to listen more closely.

"Miss. Kashner?" a male voice asks.

"Yes, that's me."

Gavin grinds his teeth.

Not recognizing the redheaded youth from any of her church activities, Elizabeth inquires after his name. He does not answer. She looks around, feeling a bit uneasy. "Do we know each other?"

He does not answer.

She grows frustrated. "How do you know my name?"

"I'm Stephen Winters. I was the one who hit Justin."

Gavin, still hiding in aisle seven, takes a step back. He could just walk out. After all, no one would know he was even there, but then he hears a loud thud. He turns the corner and sees the young man from the accident hovering over Elizabeth on the floor. "What's going on?" Gavin demands, hurrying toward them.

"I hit Justin," Stephen says, seeming unsure of what to do.

Gavin ignores the teenager. He directs his attention to Elizabeth who blinks a few times, coming around. She offers him a stream of expressions: disbelief, puzzlement, and then relief. He turns his head to escape her gaze and pulls her up. She leans against him, relying on his strength. Unexpectedly, he does not find this disagreeable.

"I must have slipped on the paper towel roll," Elizabeth explains, placing her hand to her forehead in an attempt to try and stop the room from spinning.

Gavin points at the deep gash on Elizabeth's arm. "It looks like you really hurt yourself."

"Yeah, I think I hit the cart on the way down."

Gavin grabs the roll off the floor. Unwinding and discarding the papers into the cart that had been exposed to the floor, he tears off a clean towel and reaches for Elizabeth's arm. Clasping it, he feels her body shaking. He forgoes any kind of reassurance and keeps to dabbing at the wound.

"Is she going to be okay?" Stephen asks.

"I think she'll survive," Gavin offers.

"I've really messed this up," Stephen says, turning away. He then looks at Elizabeth, seeming to gain some control. "I wanted you to know that I came to his funeral."

Elizabeth keeps her focus on her arm.

"I came because I needed to talk to you," he explains seeming undeterred. "I went to your house too, this morning, but I left." He takes a step closer. "Both times I just couldn't figure out what to say or even if I had any right to say anything. Nothing seemed good enough."

Stephen places his hands on both sides of his head as his eyes begin to water. "You see, I can't get it out of my head," he says nearly sobbing causing Elizabeth to look up. "You must forgive me, Miss Kashner," he puts his hand to his chest, "because I cannot forgive myself."

Elizabeth glances at Gavin, hoping for some kind of suggestion on what to say, but he only shakes his head, barely raising his eyes.

The idea was preposterous, of course. Why should she forgive him? Someone had to take responsibility for what had happened. She looks away and sees the open bag of cheese puffs in her cart, and she remembers the other person involved in the accident and the countless times she had told him to look both ways as he rode that bike of his. He was often reckless on it—head in the clouds—oblivious to everything around him.

She glances again at the youth. When she had first heard of the accident, she had constructed in her mind the type of person who had hit Justin. She knew from the paper that he had been a 19 year old named Stephen Winters. In reading the article, she had imagined a teenager hooked on drugs or alcohol—roughed up and battered from an undisciplined life, with the accident being just another crime added to a long list of offenses. But this Stephen Winters was the opposite of what she had considered. He seemed remorseful for an accident that, if she were honest with herself, was no one's fault. He was also displaying a kind of maturity and courageousness too. After all, it had taken both to come and say what he was saying to her now.

"You said you came to the funeral?" Elizabeth finally says.

He shakes his head and wipes his eyes. "From listening to everyone there, Justin seemed to love the outdoors. I think we would have gotten along because of that." He laughs slightly. "That story about him going fishing with his grandpa for the first time and knowing all the names of the fishes reminded me of myself."

"He was proud of himself for knowing all those different names," Elizabeth offers, remembering, and in recollecting, she must have smiled, for Stephen's expression improved as well.

To Gavin, the scene seems to drag on forever. He points at Stephen. "Go to the first aid aisle, and get some antiseptic, gauze, and first aid tape."

Stephen dabs at his eyes with his sleeve and hurries down the aisle.

"I was there; I get that it was an accident," Gavin utters to Elizabeth, "but you can't tell me that you actually feel like forgiving him for what he did."

"I don't," Elizabeth offers, wiping away her own tears, "but sometimes you can't trust the way you feel."

Gavin coughs roughly and looks away, understanding that the comment was partially meant for him. "I just hope that kid gets some driving lessons."

"Please don't tell anyone about this, Gavin. I don't want my family to hear about it from anyone else but me."

"Don't worry; I've grown accustom to keeping secrets."

Without shifting his attention from the manila folder within his hands, Juan closes the examination room door. "Hmm," he offers and flips a page over the folder. "Hmm," he hums again, which for Juan could mean either something good or something bad. "There's nothing wrong with you, Gavin," Juan declares, slapping the folder down on the small desk that was beside the examination table.

Juan Gutierrez had been Gavin's friend since college. Juan, the dedicated senior, was known for staying up all night studying, while only occasionally taking a break to play a game of cards or to buy a new designer tie. Gavin, the freshman, on the other hand had spent much of his year playing pranks and getting mediocre grades.

"What's this all about?" Juan asks, slipping his hands into his pockets. "A week and a half ago, you came in here asking for all kinds of tests. You were barely coherent. Now, if I may say you're much calmer. In fact, there seems to be something different about you all together. You seem more confident, one might say even a bit cocky.

"I guess I'm starting to get used to the idea."

"To what idea?"

"Nice leather shoes, Juan. Are they Italian?"

"Gavin? What idea?"

"Got something sharp?"

"Why?"

"Give me something sharp."

Juan turns around to one of the drawers under the counter. He pulls out a scalpel and hands it to Gavin.

Gavin opens his hand, looks at Juan, and slashes at his palm.

Juan grasps his friend's hand. "What are you doing?" He examines the wound and then spins around to the counter again. When he turns back with some antiseptic, he searches for the gash. "It was this hand, right?"

"Yes."

Juan seems to ignore the answer and looks over Gavin's other hand. His professionalism deteriorates, and he stumbles back into his chair.

"How do you explain that, Dr. Juan?"

"Let me see that again," Juan asks like a child at the fair, seeming to allow his curiosity to trump his many years at medical school.

Accepting the request, Gavin slices his hand from thumb to middle finger. He grimaces slightly as he twists his wrist around for Juan to see. A few drops of blood hit the floor, and then, as if it were a zipper, the wound closes shut.

"Whoa."

"I had hoped for a more professional diagnosis, Juan." Juan moves closer and then examines Gavin's eyes. "You don't feel like eating people, do you?"

Gavin pushes Juan's hands away. "I'm not a zombie, Juan. Besides I'm not even sure I die when I really get injured. I just get knocked unconscious."

"What do you mean, 'when you really get injured'?"

"Well, I might have fallen down a set of stairs."

Juan gives him a look of general curiosity.

"It ended up being an accident in the end, but it started out being a way for me to see what it was all about. Professor Brickley believes that God is healing me."

"Hmm," Juan sounds.

Gavin slides off the examination table. "Thanks, Juan. It's been fun."

Juan shakes his head as if he were attempting to discard his amazement. "You and I both went to college, right?"

"Yeah."

"And we probably spent about $100,000 between us for the privilege."

"That sounds about right."

"And the one basic thing that we probably learned there was that life is a mystery." Juan sends his hand through his hair, "maybe they were right."

"Not that I really would have done it, but at least we know now that I could have survived that jump off Manchester Hall."

Juan laughs, remembering. "Yeah, I could have won big on that bet."

"I'd like to keep this a secret, Juan," Gavin states, anticipating Juan's next question, which more than likely had something to do with money.

"Of course, I'll keep it to myself, but you wouldn't mind me running a few more tests?"

"I'm not becoming your guinea pig, Juan."

"Okay, okay, I thought I'd at least ask. But remember," he says, placing his hand on Gavin's shoulder, "there's always the circus."

Gavin scoffs at this and walks out into the hall while Juan follows. "You will let me know if anything changes," Juan requests.

"Nothing will change."

Chapter 6

Elizabeth stands at the far end of a long corridor. The room is dim, lit only by the upturned sconces that highlight the plaster work where the wall meets the ceiling.

Before her, a granite-topped registration desk is rich with swirls of red and gold. It cools her arm as she leans against it. She smiles at the attendant manning the counter. In return, he offers her a polite nod as he resumes his phone conversation. "I will make sure that your comments are brought to the manager's attention," he says. The attendant pauses as the person on the other end speaks.

Elizabeth begins to collect the pens and pencils that are scattered across the counter, placing them in front of her.

"No, I'm afraid the manager is not in at the moment, but I will be sure to forward your concerns to him."

Another long pause.

"Yes, I apologize. Yes, I understand. Again I do apolo—no, the manager is not in, but he will receive your complaints. Yes, goodbye." He places the receiver down and immediately turns to Elizabeth. She half expects him to make a snide remark about the caller. Instead he asks her how he can help.

"I'm looking for banquet room D," Elizabeth replies.

"Ah, yes. Our signs are not quite done yet. Please allow me to escort you to the banquet room."

He moves around the desk and ushers her down one of the corridors that is connected to the centralized registration room. They pass by an upscale shop, displaying items of glass and silver. She turns her gaze to the other side of the hall and finds a wide doorway, which leads into the hotel's only restaurant.

Admiring the ornate Victorian architecture, Elizabeth slows her pace. The hotel was a bit too fancy for her and her casual family, but her friend Trish, who loved anything that was lavish and elegant, had arranged the party.

"A wonderful restoration job," the attendant states with pride.

"Yeah, I love to see buildings like this come back to life." Elizabeth scans the room. Everyone seemed to be dressed in their best attire. She admires the scene before letting her attention come to rest on a single table in the middle of the room. With his jet black hair and tailored suit, the lighting, the setting, and the way he was slouching in his seat, Gavin looked like a romanticized version of himself.

"Would you care to look at the menu for future reference?" the attendant asks, probably curious as to why she had stopped.

"No, I just saw someone I recognized." Elizabeth motions at the restaurant. "I think I'll say hi."

"Of course, Banquet Room D is the next room on the left."

Elizabeth betters her posture and puts right the sleeve of her dress that had upturned itself on her shoulder. Slowing her stride from her usual pace of a race horse to a more feminine speed, she keeps her focus squarely on her destination. Her attention is so fixed, however, that she does not notice a waitress coming right at her with a drink tray. They nearly collide.

The commotion causes Gavin to glance up from his menu. He mumbles something under his breath as Elizabeth grabs hold of the empty chair at his table.

"Elizabeth."

She smiles at him brightly. "Sorry," she says, with a nervous laugh. "I was on my way to a party and noticed you from the hall. I thought I'd stop and thank you for your help at the grocery store. I don't think I actual did thank you." She holds up her arm for him to see. "As you can see, the scrape is healing nicely."

Gavin closes his menu and pushes it across the table. "I'm glad," he offers with a tone that contradicted his words.

Elizabeth sits down at the table. "The party is actually a going-away party," she explains.

"For?"

"For me."

"And where is it that you are going away to?"

"To the land of the Ninevites," Elizabeth answers, laughing. "No it's to Russia, the Russian republic of Ingushetia actually. It's a missionary trip. Juan helped me find the group I'm going with. We're distributing hygiene kits, bags of clothes, and blankets provided by a few churches and, from what I am told, one very wealthy benefactor. Then we're moving on to the home of a man to help set up a local Christian education program."

"And how long will you be gone?"

"About four months—get in, get out is the schedule of things in a region where foreigners are not looked on all too favorably."

Gavin moves in closer, "Why are you disturbing the nice people of Russia with your Americanized Christianity, Elizabeth? Just leave them be."

Elizabeth looks away, toward the large windows at the far end of the restaurant. The glass panes were merely black squares now due to the growing darkness outside.

"The truth is, I really don't want to go, but I don't think I'll have any peace until I do." Elizabeth waits for a response. Not getting one, she glances up at the large chandeliers. "This place really is beautiful. Isn't it?"

"Yes, I understand the rooms are quite nice," Gavin answers, folding his hands neatly together on the table. "How about after your party we go and check one out."

"That's real funny, Gavin."

Gavin does not look at her face. He already knows what he will find there if he did. Only after she is gone does he look up from the table.

He leans back toward a gentleman at the table behind him. "People just keep walking out on me lately. I have no idea why."

CHAPTER 7

Her gaze is pointed, focused—her mind, highly alert. She is aware of every sound, every movement of the plane. The armrest beside her and the pillow nestled behind her, both intended to be objects of comfort, provide none. She hates the flight attendants, particularly the one with the long black hair, exotic look about her, and perpetual smile.

Her stomach feels as if it were collapsing within her. She goes for her medicine but then realizes that she did not pack it in her carry-on. *Please help me, God.*

This fear of traveling was a new obstacle for Elizabeth, originating most likely from her sister's car accident that had ended her life. Despite this phobia, she believed she had to take this trip.

The Russian missionary who had visited her church was the last connection in a long string of encounters that had compelled her to think she should go. Uncertain, however, she had pushed the thought aside and battled the persistent call.

She argued that her job at church allowed her to do God's work. She had done well at her duties of coordinating Bible classes, researching curriculum, and on occasion speaking on some topic in front of the women of the church. It was comfortable, it was familiar, and she thought that it would satisfy the desire within her to evangelize. She thought it would satisfy God. But something was still arguing the other side within her.

Scribed on a plaque behind her desk was a quote from C.T. Studd, a missionary who had gone to China to preach the Gospel and who later gave away his inheritance. The sign had been a graduation present from a proud grandfather who liked the idea of his granddaughter venturing into the jungle to spread the Word of God. Little did he know that his granddaughter would end up at a desk job, two miles from home.

The quote's ever-present chant seemed to verify what she was feeling from God. A one sided audible conversation ensued over the next few weeks:

Week 1 - "No, I'm not going."
Week 1 ½ - "I don't want to go."
Week 2 - "Why do you want me to go?"
Week 3 - "You really want me to go?"
Week 4 - "Okay, I'll go."

Within her mind's world, safe behind her desk, it seemed wonderful to be used like this, but when the trip was placed on the calendar and the day came to purchase the plane tickets, again her fear overpowered her.

Her hands immobile now, they tingle as if asleep. She begins to breathe like a woman in labor. The man next to her smiles as if he understood. She immediately dislikes him. What business is it of his anyway? *Oh, I'm sorry. Please help me, God.*

She begins to then worry about what is ahead of her, the work that she would be doing, it's unpredictability, and the unsteadiness of its pattern. *Oh, these thoughts.* The plane then takes on the size and shape of a prison cell. She unbuckles her belt and slides to the edge of her seat. She wants to tear out of it and run screaming up and down the aisles. *No, I can't do that. They will shoot me.*

Tears cloud her eyes. Then the thought of what is ahead of her, far ahead of her, seems to be placed in her mind. It puts everything into perspective. She lays her hand on her chest. She can feel her heart beginning to slow. Laying her head back, she eventually drifts off to sleep.

⅄

Her hosts for the weeklong orientation session in England turn out to be both warm and welcoming. She almost wishes they weren't. In anticipation of having an American in their midst, it seemed that they had stocked up on every tradi-tional food ever concocted by the British.

At breakfast, feeling a bit jetlagged, she is met with a black hole next to her egg.

"Black pudding," Phillip, the man of the house, informs her while pointing with his knife, "you won't find that back in the States."

She wanted to tell him that she hadn't been looking for it back in the States.

At lunch she is relieved at the sight of two pieces of toast on her plate. She waits for a list of cold cuts, but then a ladle of hot beans is spread across her toast.

"You do know, don't you, that this was a British and American collabora-tion?" Phillip asks her as he forks a bite full into his mouth.

Before dinner, she is prepared with an apology and walks her timid stomach down to a local inn. She orders fish and holds the chips. The man behind the counter gives her an odd look.

She takes a seat and notices a young couple across the street huddled to-gether under an umbrella. They peer into a display window at a piece of modern sculpture. They scurry into the shop, disappearing through the darkened door-way, apparently happy in deciding to take the item home. Like that sculpture, Elizabeth wished she could go to where Justin was now, bundle him up, and take him home again.

On the first day she had ever seen him, he had been so small and fragile. Always needing a little bit more, he had given back to her what she never thought she needed. Born a nephew, he later became a son.

But had she been a good substitute parent? The children's mother and father had died when both boys were too young to remember, but the lack of some-thing was ever present in their eyes. Somehow, with such a tragic beginning to his life, Justin had grown into a fun-loving child.

The death of her sister and brother-in-law had brought about other things as well. The car accident had caused Elizabeth to consider her own mortality, eventually leading her to stand in a line outside a convention center where Gavin had literally handed her the ticket that had led to her salvation.

It was incredible that someone who had been so integral to her life was no longer residing within it. Blurred memories, which with time were becoming even more so, were the only proof that he had ever existed there.

She had to be honest. She missed him—maybe even more than Justin, for the possibility was always there that Gavin could someday, somehow, reenter her life and take up his place beside her.

CHAPTER 8

Five days later and one surprisingly uneventful plane ride into Vladikavkaz, North Ossetia, Elizabeth and her group are instructed to wait by a four door sedan.

Maria points at the model name on the car, "Do you know what that means?" she asks with her strong French accent getting in the way.

"I don't know, but it should mean, little," Elizabeth responds.

The man whose task it was to drive the group to the camp squeezes Maria and two others into the sedan. He points his greasy finger at Elizabeth, making her his fourth. She looks back at the security team's spacious vehicle and wonders if she should make a dash for it.

A few minutes into the car ride, she wishes she were back flying the unfriendly Russian skies. At least in the air, there were no roads, but then again, there were really no roads here either—just mere suggestions as to where one should go around the enormous holes. To make matters worse, their driver was either awful at driving or brilliant at avoiding potential security hazards. Signs are neglected. Lights are ignored. Other drivers are given hand gestures instead of the right-of-way.

"Being from a small town in Pennsylvania," Elizabeth says to no one in particular, "where most of the population consists of quiet inhabitants of German ancestry, this kind of driving is a bit of a shock." Her words bounce out of her as the car wobbles down the uneven road. "Back home, you simply grit your teeth or said a swear word under your breath if someone's driving annoyed you. And only in the most extreme cases did you ever blow your horn."

The comment seems to go unnoticed, but then again so does the request from the director, Dyson Stewart to pull over and relieve himself. "I knew there were hostage takers in this country, but this is ridicules," Dyson jokes, making the group laugh and only partially easing the tension boiling up in the car. The driver, apparently well versed in the English language, pays no attention to the exchange and continues to pass car after car. Elizabeth closes her eyes and prays for a stronger constitution.

As they approach the camp, she looks the place over. One of the largest refugee camps in Ingushetia, it appears less crowded than it had in the film that they had viewed in orientation. In the video, Dyson had led the camera through the muddy avenues, pointing to tent after tent where occupants battled Tuberculosis. Plump women, with head scarves knotted tightly under their chins or behind their heads, had gathered together and stared at the camera. They had looked cold, worried and disheartened as children ran around them, amused by the sight of the video equipment.

The production moved on to an interview with an elderly woman who gave a tour of her family's tent. The cloth structure had a woman's touch everywhere, from the flowered patterned sheets used as wallpaper to the vase of plastic roses displayed on a humble wooden table.

The scene illustrated the natural need of women to make a home wherever they found themselves. Elizabeth was doing the very same thing, arranging family photographs whenever she found a bedside table to place them on.

The driver parks the car near a row of tents that were no different from the rest of the tents throughout the camp. The team stumbles out of the car and huddles in a circle, seeming apprehensive to venture any farther than their group.

"Only if asked," Dyson had answered after a question about witnessing had been posed to him during orientation. "But in order to be asked, you must build a relationship."

He then had looked down at his paper, seeming to think for a moment about how to phrase his next set of words. "In all honesty, those on the medical team, who will have more direct access to the people, will have more of a chance to do this than the rest of us. But we will still be serving, if only indirectly.

"If, however, God works within someone and they do ask you questions about your faith, respond cautiously," Dyson had warned. "You are going to a people who, in just a few years, have witnessed the fall of the Soviet Union as well as two wars with Russia. They have seen a lot of hardship, and their loyalty may be with those who work against Russia and foreigners.

"And because of the help that you will be providing and the strong feelings you may have for what you are doing, you may be tempted to align yourself with those who claim to fight for these people. The Chechen warrior, however, fights either knowingly or naively for Islamists or for some criminal element that gains its power from selling drugs, weapons dealing and human trafficking.

"Remember, this place didn't just let the devil through the back door; it invited him in through the front, asked him to sit down, and have tea. So you may find opportunities to witness with some due to their bitterness with all of this, but again, do so cautiously."

Dyson's words were a sober warning that made Elizabeth, as she glances around the camp again, feel justifiably uneasy. She considers that perhaps for the trip, she should have packed a wig and a pair of sunglasses.

Dyson steps out from the team. "We are fortunate to be here. With the goal of wanting to shut the camps down, the officials have been making it more and more difficult for aid personnel to have access to them, but once again, it has come down to who you know," he says, smiling.

"I have some rules to go over again. First rule—never leave the camp. If you need to leave the camp, discuss it with me, and we will set something up with the escort." He points at the security team's parked vehicle. "Second rule—If you are going to leave your work station, do so with a partner. As we touched on in orientation, kidnapping is big business here, and as a foreigner, you equate to a larger ransom. As we travel, this will be more of a worry, but this camp, despite its police and military personnel, still has its dangers."

A man in a wrinkled jacket walks up to the group, placing his hand on Dyson's shoulder. "We will discuss rule number one later, yes?"

Dyson grins and turns to the group. "Team, this is Dr. William Sweitzler. A doctor with as much dedication would be difficult to find."

Dr. Sweitzler pats Dyson on the back, "Vielen dank." He points at the team. "May I?"

"Yes, of course." Dyson takes a step back.

Forgoing any eye contact, Dr. Sweitzler looks over heads and at the spaces between the members. "You are all aid workers. You have not the luxury to be on anyone's side. You are on the side of life; death is your enemy." His words are edged with a slight German accent and seem disingenuousness as if he were merely reading from a textbook. "You are here to preserve human lives," he continues, this time with more sincerity. "That is your purpose. It is not to convert the entire population." He grins slightly as Patricia, one of the nurses on the team, shakes her head in agreement. He offers her full eye contact. "I will show your team around. We will get started now."

Dr. Sweitzler leads the team through the doors of one of the only two substantial buildings in the camp. Entering into the main room, it becomes clear that it has been turned into a kind of makeshift medical center.

The women are then led to the other building, the men to a tent. "Get settled. Go to bed," Dr. Sweitzler commands, keeping his view to the ceiling.

⅄

Elizabeth clobbers her travel alarm clock, killing the squealer. It was 5:00 AM. Someone was probably given a fairly good salary to decide what kind of noise went into alarm clocks; she wished she knew where they lived.

Shedding the covers from over her head, she looks around. She is in a small building, that much she knew. The rest was a little foggy, if not a bit bizarre. Remembering completely, she creeps back down into her sleeping bag.

A clanging noise coming from the other end of the building breaks through the silence, causing Elizabeth to crawl from her hiding place. She sees Maria, staring at a pot of coffee brewing on top of their heater-stove.

Layering on another pair of socks, Elizabeth moves quietly in the direction of the aroma, using the narrow aisle that was formed by two rows of four cots on either side. She advances more quickly as Maria pours out a full cup.

"Good morning," Elizabeth says to Maria.

"Bonjour," Maria answers softly, handing Elizabeth a mug.

Maria takes a few more sips herself then turns in the direction of the cots. "GET UP," she orders like some Admiral of the Fleet commanding a group of ships at war. Elizabeth shifts away, raising an eyebrow. Complete mayhem commences.

The night before, it had been decided among the women that the camp's bathhouses would be avoided at all costs until it became inescapable to do so. Instead, the women performed their pared-down morning beauty routines, many of which began with a wet wipe and ended with a pony tail.

Elizabeth goes through her own routine. She grabs a mug of boiling water and heads outside. She brushes her teeth and looks at the white glow of the Caucasus Mountains. They make an impression, causing her to feel small, but not insignificant. She thanks God for the reminder, recalling a certain conversation with one of the youth group members at her church. "If God is all-knowing," the boy had asked, "what's the point of evangelizing? I mean if God knows who is going to be saved, why bother?" His tone had been slightly desperate as if any item in the Bible left unexplained could put an end to his whole enterprise of believing.

"Then why bother doing anything?" she had answered him.

"Well, that's true."

"What you can be assured of is that, for whatever reason, God has called us to be a part of the process, part of the joy of sharing the Good News."

Lindsey, one of the younger team members, steps out from the building, drawing Elizabeth back to the present. "I don't think we can hold it any longer," she explains. "We're off to the bathrooms. Are you coming?"

In a tightly bond group, the women make a march toward the outhouses. Near the wooden structures, little streams have cut their way through the terrain turning the dirt to mud.

"Thank goodness we brought our boots," Elizabeth says to Lindsey as they muck their way to their chosen outhouse.

Nearly slipping in the slop, Elizabeth grasps Lindsey's hand. Their laughter ends as a man appears from behind the building. He leans up against the outhouse door while crossing his arms and looking Lindsey over.

Elizabeth realizes that Maria's imposing manner could be useful right now, but she had already gone into another outhouse. "Excuse us," Elizabeth states. The man does not move. "Excuse us," Elizabeth says this time in Russian, louder and with more force. A rattling comes from inside the outhouse, and a boy pops out the door. He takes a hold of the man's hand, and they stroll back to camp.

The women laugh at each other. Lindsey pats Elizabeth's hand and points at the outhouse. "You go first."

Inside the wooden box, it is both damp and cold, but the temperature is the least of Elizabeth's concerns. She takes short breaths not wanting to take in too much of the foul air. She tries to stand up again without using the aid of the studs covered with weird looking dead bugs. Feeling a bit triumphant back on her feet, she stumbles out of the outhouse and frowns at Lindsey, "How much can a person take?"

Lindsey chuckles.

"I know I shouldn't complain," Elizabeth admits.

"That's very true, Elizabeth. Now, wish me luck," Lindsey hops into the outhouse and in less than a minute jumps back out. "I think as it gets colder, I'll get faster."

"I don't know how that would be possible."

The line for the aid provisions winds back through the first two avenues of tents. The recipients wait patiently but seem embarrassed by the donations. Elizabeth begins to suffer the same discomfort. She fixes a smile on her face, trying to mask the feeling.

"How's it going?" Dyson asks, coming up behind her. She does not answer, and he gives her a knowing look. He turns to the next set of people in line and begins to converse and laugh with them as if he were merely talking with his neighbors back home.

Elizabeth nods her head. "That seemed to do the trick."

"They are a proud people."

"Aren't we all," Elizabeth states, placing a hygiene kit in the hands of a young woman. She then turns back to Dyson. "I suppose some people would think we're crazy for coming here."

Dyson tears open another box of supplies. "And to those people, I would say that they would be crazy if they were to come here. But you shouldn't try to live someone else's life. I tried that once, and it didn't work out too well," Dyson confesses, placing the supplies on the table in neat short rows. "Picture it, me in a business suit working at a bank."

"You're kidding, right?" Elizabeth responds.

"I'm afraid not."

"You were really off course, weren't you?"

"I was, but I still get a lot of discouraging words about what we are trying to do here." Dyson says, roughly scratching the side of his head. "Some complain that the volunteer's motives are less than pure. And I couldn't disagree with that. Some people do come here because they are running from something or because they have something to prove." He lets out a long exhale. "The truth is, I could care less why they're here—let God sort that out. Just as long as they work hard and get the job done, I'm glad to have them."

Elizabeth could see a kind of weariness in Dyson, a weariness, that she guessed, stemmed from a reality of having too few workers and very little time for idealistic motivations. Dyson hid his fatigue well. It remained concealed behind his natural charisma and enthusiasm.

"So what do you do for fun, Elizabeth?" Dyson asks, seeming to want to change the subject to something less serious.

"I like to garden."

"Okay," he responds seeming unimpressed.

"And go target shooting. I took it up after one particularly bad performance involving a bug."

CHAPTER 9

At the edge of the encampment, a group of kids play a game of soccer in the evening light. As Elizabeth walks by, their laughter causes her to pause. The youngsters run around and kick at the ball seemingly just for fun without any strategy in mind.

"Are you coming, Elizabeth?" Lindsey turns around to inquire.

"I'll be along."

Maria and Lindsey look at each other and hesitate.

"Don't worry. I'll be all right."

Elizabeth settles on a grassy spot near the border of the game. She listens to the laughter and begins collecting small pebbles off the ground. Justin loved hunting for stones and rocks, she recalls. Standing on his little kitchen stool, he would wash them in the sink, until their true colors would come through. Often she would find one or two left behind, floating in a dirty coffee mug.

Next to her foot, she finds a burgundy one. She picks it up and then another and another. She lets them fall through her fingers. She better stop. She did not want to end up like her Aunt Annie whose house, after the death of her husband, took on the appearance of a storage unit.

Looking out into the field, she notices a young boy emerging from the game. He collapses on the grass beside her. Rubbing his forehead with the back of his hand, he says something in the Chechen language.

"Are you okay?" she asks out of habit, realizing as soon as the words leave her mouth that the boy probably will not understand her.

The child lifts his head. "You speak English?"

"Yes…and it sounds like you do too."

"Does my English sound, ah…okay?"

Elizabeth shivers a little from the cold breeze. "So far so good."

"My father taught me English. He thought it was good for me to know, but I cannot remember why."

"Why don't you ask him?"

"I cannot…he is dead."

Elizabeth looks toward the mountains. "I'm sorry," she replies knowing that she could say more on the topic of death and loss, but feeling a kind of tiredness within her, she simply decides not to.

The boy outlines the peaks of the mountains with his finger. "My father liked to paint. He enjoyed mountains as…a subject?"

Elizabeth nods. "That's correct."

"Do you mind if I, ah…practice speaking English with you?"

"What is your name?"

"Ovlur."

A burst of chilly air needles Elizabeth's face and mouth. "Well, Ovlur, my name is Elizabeth, and I'd be happy to help you."

The following evening's job is a 3D puzzle—a project of moving all the leftover supplies into an already overcrowded storage shed. Elizabeth picks up the next box that needs positioned into the shack. She scratches her forehead in order to stall, knowing that Dyson was beginning to get a bit compulsive about the task.

"Elizabeth, can I help?" Ovlur asks, scurrying up to them.

"Certainly, Ovlur," Elizabeth replies.

"There." He points at a spot where her box would fit perfectly.

Dyson smiles at Elizabeth. "I see you've met Ovlur."

"Oh, you know each other?"

"He's pretty famous around here—always willing to help. I've often wished there were more than one of him."

"Are there any more of you, Ovlur?" Elizabeth asks.

Ovlur wipes his nose with the back of his hand. "No, I don't think so."

Elizabeth laughs. "You are unique."

"What does u-nique mean?"

"It means something is one of a kind. There is nothing else like it," Elizabeth answers.

"The socks my friend made me are unique." Ovlur draws his pant leg up to show that he has used the word correctly.

"Yes, they are definitely unique," Elizabeth says with a grin.

As the last box is stored away, Ovlur runs away to play the day's final game of soccer. Dyson asks the group to gather together to go over the next day's schedule. Elizabeth only half listens. The talk of traveling on to their next destination only serves to unnerve her.

Dyson ends with a prayer and then motions to Elizabeth. "Would you walk with me?"

"Of course."

As they start out, there is a bit of small talk about the trip, and then Dyson's tone changes, "It might not seem so, but Ovlur is a troubled young man. I think his father's disappearance is to blame—among other things." Dyson looks away, burrowing his hands into the pockets of his lightweight jacket. "I think he helps because it helps. You know?"

"I do." Elizabeth slides her gloves on. "But I thought his father had passed away."

Dyson stares at her for a moment, "that all depends on who's telling the story."

"Oh?"

"Like I said, Ovlur is rather famous around here but that has more to do with his father than with Ovlur's personality. At least for the refugees from the mountain regions, Ovlur's father is a bit of a legend. There is a story they tell." Dyson stops. "It's rather gruesome."

"I think at this point you better just tell me," she instructs, stepping closer.

Dyson grimaces a bit. "Well, it was during the second war between the Chechens and the Russians. Ovlur's father, Dasha, had been tracking a unit of Russian soldiers moving through the woods for days. One night it started to snow. At first, it was just a light snow, but it just kept coming. For the soldiers, with their run-down, heavy vehicles, the terrain had been difficult to negotiate even without the snow, but now with the bad weather, they soon found themselves trapped. So they settled in and waited. And so did Dasha.

"In the dead of night, he took advantage of the situation. He slit the throats of twelve men before anyone even realized it. The Russians, probably embarrassed by the fact that one man had killed twelve of their own, claimed that Dasha had frozen to death as he retreated, but the locals didn't buy it. They knew that Dasha was familiar with the mountains well enough to have survived. They say he's still alive, roaming them to this day."

Dyson peers at the black sky and lets out a cloud of air. "I worry that, because of this history, Ovlur will get caught up in one of these groups that you hear about in the region. I've talked to him about it. I hope he takes the advice."

Back at her quarters, after hearing Dyson's account of Ovlur's father, Elizabeth is glad for the brief conversations that pop up here and there between the women. They were a good distraction, for the short discussions revealed odd, little ways in which the women's lives were connected.

Two have family origins from Poland. Four loved the movie *Suspicion*, with Cary Grant, and have seen it a million times. One knows a Joe Harper from a small town in Canada, and another grew up remembering his father of the same name. Three have reptiles as pets.

As Elizabeth listens, she recalls something she had learned at orientation, how during the Middle Ages, missionaries from Georgia had crossed into what was today Chechnya and attempted to establish the Christian faith among its pagan inhabitants. The Christian influence did not endeavor long, however, as the Mongolian invasion severed ties between the converted pagans and their Georgian Christian neighbors, causing many of the converts to return to their pagan ways. Christianity then all but disappeared as Islam began to take hold. To Elizabeth, the lesson was clear: human connections were important. Lost or won they often came with an eternal consequence.

The volume increases in the room. Chatter fills the corners. No longer able to hear individual conversations, Elizabeth loses interest. "Anyone up for a walk?" she says, feeling as if her words had hit an invisible wall and bounced back at her.

She tightens her scarf and makes her way to the door. As she goes, Maria offers to tag along, but Elizabeth has already decided to go alone. "I'm just going to the other building."

Closing the door behind her, she notices that her hand has become wet from the night's dew on the doorknob. She looks out at the snow-capped mountains glowing in the darkness. So quiet is the night that a need to pray comes over her.

In the vastness of the outdoors, her words float up toward the atmosphere and beyond, unimpeded by wall or ceiling. The sensation distracts her for a moment, and she is in awe. In the dark, cold night she just stands there waiting for a voiced response, like Moses had the good fortune of receiving, but she knows Moses had it easy. Well, sort of anyway. Turning inward but finding no change in her attitude, she takes a deep breath. Tiredness overcomes her, and she runs out of words.

She slows her pace as she draws closer to the other building. Stepping onto the wooden stoop, she overhears Dyson talking, "You come very close to defending fanatics like Kuyara."

"Terrorists want me dead, yes?" William replies. "I can respect that."

Dyson laughs. "I will never understand you, William."

Elizabeth pauses for a moment waiting to see if the conversation between the two men will continue, but hearing only silence, she opens the door.

Dyson scrutinizes her as he tosses a bunch of papers onto a nearby desk. "Elizabeth, you're breaking rule number two," he says, looking more worried than he needed to.

"I wanted a break from the land of women."

Dyson's expression softens. "William, this is Elizabeth Kashner."

Dr. Sweitzler takes her hand and gives it a solid shake. "What has led you to this place, Elizabeth?"

"God," Elizabeth answers with a smile.

Dr. Sweitzler places a cigarette between his lips. "So you were dragged here, yes?"

She laughs, "Pretty much."

"What do you think God intends to do with you while you are here?"

"William, leave her alone," Dyson utters from the corner of the room.

Elizabeth pauses but then continues, "Well, if I have to eat any more of those freeze-dried food packs, I will think it was to lose weight."

Dr. Sweitzler examines the cigarette in his hand. "So you are not one of these zealous Christians who craves spreading the Good News?"

"Well, you know us Evangelicals; we just can't help ourselves."

"Good luck with that," Dr. Sweitzler smirks and then steps outside.

"Just ignore him," Dyson suggests and then motions to her to come closer. She maneuvers around the desk, coming to stand beside him.

"I want you to have something. I want you to have my gun."

"Your gun?" Elizabeth questions.

Studying her for a moment, he reaches under his jacket and pulls out a holstered handgun that was hidden beneath his coat. He extracts the magazine from the weapon, checks the chamber, and with the muzzle facing down, hands the firearm to her. "I just…" he begins, trailing off.

"What?"

"I just wanted you to have it, and after our talk the other day, I know you can handle it."

"It's illegal."

"Of course, but it's a lot better than that aerosol gun you told me you had."

"I'm not taking your gun, Dyson," Elizabeth protests.

"Here's the magazine and holster. I know you said you shot one of these before, but you may want to do some dry firing to practice your trigger control."

"Dyson," Dr. Sweitzler shouts, poking his head through the door but not looking directly at them. A cigarette, half burnt, hangs precariously on his lower lip. "They are taking Kuyara's brother away," he explains, letting out a ball of smoke that unravels as Dyson marches through its cloudy white strings.

"Who's Kuyara?" Elizabeth asks just before Dyson steps out the door.

Dyson turns, seeming upset.

"I sort of overheard you talking about him before I came in," Elizabeth confesses.

Dyson rubs at his brow. "Let's just say he's someone I've been trying to… rehabilitate." Dyson smiles weakly. "Remember that type has a safe action trigger," he utters, pointing at his gun still within her hand.

"Dyson," she replies, but he ignores her and continues out the door.

From inside, Elizabeth watches as three figures pass through the light from the office. The center figure turns to look at her. His arms form a V behind his back, and metal handcuffs on his wrists glint as the trio passes through the light's illumination.

After returning the magazine to the gun, Elizabeth conceals the holstered weapon under her jacket. She then trails along Dyson's path and ends her journey near a group of spectators gathered outside the building.

"They accused Kuyara's brother of terrorism," Dr. Sweitzler explains to Elizabeth. "Family refutes this. It is of no matter. Russians do not care. They do not need reason to take these people's sons. They just take them."

"You seem to have chosen a side, Dr. Sweitzler."

"Do not be naive, Elizabeth. Everyone is on a side. You being on the worst side of all—hoping that after the military has cleared the way, you will convert the rest with your prayers."

Dyson, standing on the other side of William, points to a man advancing toward the trio. "Kuyara." Dyson steps out from the group, placing himself in Kuyara's way. Without diverting from his chosen course, Kuyara raises something at Dyson's head. A pop sounds. Dyson drops. Kuyara runs ahead.

Dr. Sweitzler propels forward as if he has done this a thousand times. Elizabeth is motionless. Time accelerates, but she remains still as if trapped in a photograph. "Oh no," she finally whispers.

"Er lebt noch!" Dr. Sweitzler shouts to the onlookers and then shakes his head. "He is still alive!" He whips out a handkerchief and presses it to the wound.

Another pop sounds and then a succession of bangs; the crowd runs in a multitude of directions. Elizabeth sees Kuyara retreating, firing his weapon erratically at two camp police, who are close behind.

She is right in his path. He begins to raise his gun at her, but she has already done the same. She aims and fires just as something zips past her ear. She grabs her right leg and yells. Kuyara runs past seemingly unharmed.

Elizabeth is halfway to the ground when a woman grabs her and begins to carry her toward the office. They hobble inside until the woman places Elizabeth on the office floor.

Elizabeth touches the left side of her face. It is wet—sticky. The woman says something while pointing at Elizabeth's right leg, but Elizabeth cannot make sense of it. Her pant leg is cut open, and her leg goes cold. Something is wrapped tight around it.

The woman's face is over her again. Her hair is a curly mass of red. For some reason, this irritates Elizabeth, and she turns her head to look away. The woman raises her eyes to the upper half of Elizabeth's body. "And in her left temple," the woman shouts before barking an order at an approaching nurse.

Elizabeth's vision fizzles and then goes black.

CHAPTER 10

Fats is not a fat man. His sister, Brig, however, had informed Gavin that years prior to going on some Asian inspired diet, that Fats had suffered from severe obesity, reaching a wrecking ball mass of 359 lbs.

Fats' wife, Carolyn, a high-pitched southern lady known in the South "for her magazine that showcased everything fine and hospitable" was thin and petite. "A sliver of a thing," Brig had joked in her fake but well-managed southern accent.

Gavin had recently met the couple along with Brig while purchasing a kayak at Fats' Hunting & Outdoor store. The store was an odd choice for ladylike Carolyn to operate, but Brig confided to Gavin that "beneath those good manners and crossed legs, there hid a woman yearning to chase a bear through the woods with a shotgun."

On top of an abandon highway bridge that spans across a deep gorge, Gavin waits for Fats and Carolyn. The two had invited him to go bungee jumping of all things. At first, Gavin had refused, knowing his limits as it pertained to heights, but after being told that Brig would be joining them, he had accepted, not wanting to appear a coward in front of her. In the end though, Brig had canceled due to work, and Gavin was left with an invitation that he would have rather not have accepted.

Exiting their SUV, Fats and Carolyn embrace. Fats, still a large man even after his weight loss, absorbs Carolyn into his frame. They both look over the railing into the ravine.

"Brown Water Crick is flow'n good." Fats roughs up his words as they tumble out of his mouth. "If there weren't so many factors to consider, I could dunk my head today." He grabs and shakes the railing of the bridge with his massive hands. The railing vibrates all the way down to where Gavin is leaning. Gavin steps back, feeling unbalanced. He looks over to his right as a car pulls onto the bridge.

"The college kids are here," Fats proclaims, marching toward the car and stopping midway as only one young man exits the car. "Alex, where's the rest of them?"

The twentysomething stretches and yawns. "They chickened out."

"No refunds."

"They know."

With the fewest number of words, the matter seemed settled, and Gavin returns his view to the 200 foot drop. "So tell me again that this is legal?" he asks.

"Don't worry," Fats answers, "It took forever, but I got permission."

Alex scratches at the two piercings over his eyebrow and yawns again. "The first time I did this, I got a call in the middle of the night telling me to get ready for an early morning jump. Half of us had to watch out for the cops the entire time."

"We're too old for those kinds of shenanigans," Carolyn says, rubbing Fats on the back. She then grins as if remembering just that kind of shenanigan.

They go about putting the jumping shelf in place, which provided a board to jump from away from the bridge. They then set up the motorized pulley system, which after each leap, would return them back to the bridge.

"So who's first?" Fats asks, hauling out the harnesses that would attach the jumper to the bungee cord.

There is a pause. Alex points at Gavin with a limp hand. "You can go."

A tinge of anxiety courses through Gavin. For someone who had a fear of heights as he had, playing chicken with a locomotive was one thing. Jumping off a bridge into a deep canyon was another. Of course, it was illogical that he would even have such a fear, but fear was often illogical. Wasn't it? And perhaps there was some logic to it after all that death was a journey. And it was the journey of *falling* which caused him to fear. Gavin's legs go weak at the thought of that, but before he can argue about going first, Fats hands him a chest harness and swami belt. "Come on, let's get you jumping. I can hardly wait to hear you scream."

Gavin's unsteady hands carry out the task that he had been taught during yesterday's training. And before he knew it, Fats was joining a three foot waffled rope, which was attached to the bungee cord, to Gavin's swami belt. He fastens the same kind of rope to his chest harness.

Gavin looks down the line beyond several feet of padded bumper that covered the cord connections and counts the number of bungee cords that were now linked to him. Glad to find the same four he had tallied in training, he takes a deep breath and reminds himself of what Fats had said: "If one breaks, the others will hold you." Sweat drips from Fats' brow. "Now tell me again how you're going to get back up to the bridge?" he asks.

Wanting to slow the process down a bit, Gavin hesitates and takes another deep breath. "A rope will be lowered down to me. When it reaches me, I'll attach it to the chest harness. The pulley system will then pull me back up to the bridge."

"Correct."

Gavin's weight is checked again, and Fats scribbles something down. He hands the pad to Carolyn, who nods. Fats checks the equipment, cords, and connections once more and finishes by attaching himself to a safety line. He waves for Gavin to go ahead of him.

Gavin climbs over the railing of the bridge and waits a moment for his legs to strengthen. Fats grins at him, probably noticing Gavin's tight hold on the bridge's railing. "At some point you will have to let go."

Gavin glances over at Alex who is at the tail end of yet another yawn. Gavin assures himself that the young man's attitude will change once it is his turn. Finding courage in this, Gavin releases his grasp.

"Now, step to that edge there. Make sure your toes are hanging out over the board and place the bungee cord to your side. Now, tell me again what you are going to do."

"Look ahead. Keep my hands out to the side. Push off with force in a swan dive." Gavin's mouth goes dry. His stomach churns. He closes his eyes. A slight breeze cools his face. Then, something strange happens. He studies the ravine below just to remind himself of the height, testing to see if it will generate some sense of alarm, but it does not.

After the incident with the train, Gavin had decided to forgo any other tests of similar dramatic nature concerning his newly acquired skill. Overtime, however, he had taken part in outdoor activities that he would have never before considered, allowing a kind of acceptance of his talent to begin to grow within him. But despite this acceptance that partnered with his reestablishing numbness, he had still felt some fear, including his fear of heights. Now, standing out over this deep pit, an evolution seemed to be taking place. He felt as if he were a fully evolved man. He felt indestructible.

"Three, two, one," Fats shouts, generating an echo through the valley.

On *one*, Gavin leaps. His body falls freely without obstruction. He accelerates. The trees blur into nothing more than broad strokes of brown and green. Every nerve, muscle and bone in his body feels alive. The water gets closer and closer, then he feels a gentle tug from the cord. Gavin's downward progression slows until he nearly comes to a complete stop, cradled by his seat harness. The cord draws him upwards.

This skyward movement does not last long; however, and he is soon falling down once more. Again, the rope becomes taut, but this time, he hears a snap, followed by three more. The secure, suspended feeling vanishes. He goes into a free fall. Grasping at the air around him, he searches for anything to end his descent. "Oh crap," he murmurs.

The same sentiment is repeated by Fats observing the frayed cords recoiling through the air. Fats races to the end of the bridge grabbing a backboard and first aid bag as he goes. Hurrying through the brush, he searches for a way down to the creek. He slips on a piece of slate and slides down a section of the path.

"Be careful!" Carolyn hollers as she fumbles with her cell phone. Her fingers shake as she presses 9-1-1.

Gavin's body is positioned next to a large bolder. His right arm is wedged under the large rock, preventing his body from being swept away by the steady current.

Fats emerges from the woods and charges into the water, leaving his equipment on the shore. He stumps his bulky legs through the rapids. Breathing hard, he stops to catch his breath. He watches as Gavin's arm comes free of the rock's hold, and his body is sent into the fast-moving water. Gavin bobs up and down on the waves toward his rescuer. "Okay…okay," Fats mumbles as he snatches Gavin's foot. Getting a better grip under Gavin's arms, he hauls his body toward the shore.

On the patch of beach, Fats rests the lifeless body and attempts CPR. Failing, he sits down beside his lost friend. He pounds his fist into the side of his head and stares out onto the creek. "My sister is going to hate me. She really liked you."

"She did?" Gavin mumbles.

Fats scoots away like a crab, sending pebbles up into the air. "How…you… you're dead."

"I'll have to disagree with you on that."

Fats says nothing, looking Gavin over like a mother with a new born baby. He then begins to laugh and hurls himself at Gavin, wrapping his big-boned arms around him. "It's like some kind of miracle."

"No, not really," Gavin argues, pulling his wet shirt away from his body.

"Are you in pain?"

"No."

"You're not?"

"No."

"Gavin, you've just survived quite a fall. Excuse me for saying so, but you hardly seem to have noticed."

Gavin pauses for a moment, remembering himself. "I must be in shock."

"Well, we will get you to the hospital since Carolyn has probably already called for an ambulance."

"I don't want to go to the hospital."

"Gavin, we've been given some kind of second chance here. Let's not throw it away by simply not making sure you're okay. At least let's have the paramedics check you out."

Gavin stirs up a handful of small stones. He pours them into his other hand. "I'll let them look me over, on one condition."

"Anything."

"I'd like to date your sister."

"My friend, I will drive you to the chapel!"

On the bridge, Carolyn watches as the two make their way up the mountain. As they approach, she runs to Gavin and hugs him, only letting go after Gavin pulls her arms from around him. Alex just stands there with his mouth open. Gavin wonders if the guy will ever jump again.

"Carolyn, God has once again gotten me out of a jam."

A few moments later, Fats draws the cords up to the bridge. Examining them, he says wide-eyed, handing them to Gavin, "Look at these. They all just snapped. Brand new, tested, stored correctly, triple checked cords and they just broke. It wasn't just one, it was all four."

Everyone turns and stares at Gavin.

Chapter 11

The sound of her name being called seems distant, and it is only when it is said once more that Elizabeth opens her eyes. As she does, recognition of the person standing before her is immediate.

The doctor leans over her and smiles. Her red hair is now slicked back into a tight bun. "Good morning. How do you feel? I'm Dr. Samantha Reynolds. Do you remember what happened?"

Elizabeth only manages a vague expression.

"You got caught in a crossfire. Your left temple was grazed by a bullet. Your right leg was also hit."

Elizabeth hears the words being spoken to her, but she cannot seem to draw any meaning from them.

"We expect you to recover fully. We have you on some morphine. That should help with the pain. Dr. Sweitzler will be in to see you shortly. He'll be taking over your care."

"Dyson?"

Dr. Reynolds offers a forlorn look. The air thickens. Outlines blur. And it was as if a section of script had been incorrectly edited when Dyson had offered her his gun. Why had he insisted on giving it to her? If only he had kept it for himself. With all of his knowledge, skill, and training he should have been the one to live.

"They did catch Kuyara," Dr. Reynolds' offers, patting Elizabeth on the arm. "That is something to be thankful for."

It is evening. Dr. Sweitzler positions himself at the entry way of the women's quarters. He stares at Elizabeth, giving her full eye contact. "You must forgive me, Elizabeth. I was focused on Dyson." He wearily pulls out a cigarette and a plastic lighter. "Not that it mattered." He slams the lighter down on the table next to her and pulls the cigarette from his mouth.

Elizabeth reaches for his hand.

He gives her a counterfeit grin, and with his free hand, he places the cigarette back into his mouth. He casts his gaze over Elizabeth's shoulder and then pauses. "He was like a brother to me." He snorts a cry and curses God.

Elizabeth withdraws her hand.

"You disapprove, yes?"

"You wouldn't understand."

He snatches the cigarette from his mouth. "Why? Because I am not a Christian?"

"Yes."

"But I am."

"I'm sorry," Elizabeth slumps back against her pillows, "I just didn't think... well, it's the things you say."

He rolls his cigarette between his fingers. "How is the pain?"

"It's manageable."

"You are lying."

"Okay, it hurts." Elizabeth repositions her body, hoping that the pain will ease. It does so slightly.

William wipes his hand down his face and tosses another complaint at God.

"Come on, William."

He chuckles with a tone of disbelief. "You are not without your own faults." He lifts his lighter to the end of his cigarette. The thing burns orange like a tiny campfire. "I saw what you held in your hand."

"What are you talking about?" Elizabeth's throat tightens.

"The gun, Elizabeth, the gun. How did you obtain it?"

"That's none of your business."

William draws the stick from his mouth and pours smoke into the air. "Arms dealing is a very bad thing, yes?"

Elizabeth can feel her face reddening. "I did not get it from any criminal."

"Then from whom?"

Elizabeth does not answer.

"From whom?" William smashes his cigarette into a metal bowl on the bed-side table. The cigarette stands on end for a few seconds and then topples over like a miniature scrunched car. "That is what I thought. You are so self—"

"I got it from Dyson. Okay?"

The statement seems to immobilize William for a moment. He sits himself down at the edge of an adjacent bed and says nothing. His hands begin to fidget as if he is unsure what to do with them now that he is not longer holding a cigarette.

He lifts his gaze to the ceiling. "I was once like you. Did you know that? I desired to be a missionary and a doctor—healing the flesh as well as the spirit," he utters with a slight mocking tone.

"I went to Scotland. I talked God in all the local pubs. They did not like this. Men grabbed me in one pub. They threw me to the door, still holding their beer mugs," he says, mimicking holding a glass. "I got up. I went on. But things like this kept occurring, and after a mob taunted me as I ran for my life, I felt it was all a lost cause. I grew tired of waiting on God. I dropped the healing the spirit part and focused on the flesh." William dives into the pocket of his jacket and pulls out a packet of cigarettes. "It is true, no? You pray and pray and pray and get nowhere."

"Maybe you were waiting for God in all the wrong places?"

"You mean like a Chechen refugee camp in Ingushetia?"

"Touché." Elizabeth frowns and then notices a volunteer pointing at her from the doorway. A tall heavyset man peeks in around her. "Miss Elizabeth Kashner?" the man inquires after thanking the volunteer.

William stands, blocking the man's view of Elizabeth. She weaves her hand around him. "I'm Elizabeth."

The man gently takes her hand. "I am Nikolai Dzutsev with the FSB."

Elizabeth slowly withdraws her hand.

"Excuse the interruption, but about..." from his coat, Nikolai draws out a small note pad, flips it open and glances at a page "Dyson Stewart, I will need to ask a few questions."

William gives up his spot and withdraws to a nearby window where he lights yet another cigarette.

"You are recovering?" Nikolai asks.

"Yes," Elizabeth says, barely looking at him.

"Very good." He wets a thick finger and pages through his little tablet. "I understand this incident happened outside hospital?"

"That's right."

Nikolai nods his head and clears his throat. "I am not so clear on the details. Please explain to me what happened next." He seems to study Elizabeth while awaiting an answer.

Elizabeth stalls a moment and tries to swallow. She fails, and her first couple of words come out sounding strained. "After Dyson was shot, Kuyara rushed ahead in order to free his brother. I guess he couldn't accomplish this and ran away."

"By you he then passed?"

"Yes."

Nikolai jots something down. "As your friend had, it is good you did not get in his way."

"But I did get in his way," Elizabeth blurts out before thinking.

Nikolai stares at her for a moment. "Do you mean to say that Kuyara goes on a mission to free his brother, kills anyone who gets in his way, and when you do the same thing, he does not shoot you?" He looks back at William. "This is a miracle."

Williams lets out a cough.

"You should be very thankful. It is not every day that one experiences such a thing." Nikolai writes something in his notebook.

"Yeah." Elizabeth glances at William. He shakes his head and mouths a "no". She turns back to Nikolai. "I can't let you think that."

Nikolai lifts his attention from his notebook. "What is it that you cannot let me think?"

"That it was a miracle. People never believe in miracles because of all the phony ones. I can't be a part of that. I mean I guess you could take it as a miracle, that I had what I had at the time, but it wasn't directly a miracle that Kuyara didn't shoot."

Nikolai glances at William who shrugs his shoulders. "Miss Kashner, tell me what happened."

"I had a gun."

"Ah," Nikolai articulates simply.

"I shot at Kuyara," Elizabeth adds and then places her hand to her temple. "I missed because I got caught in the crossfire."

William drops his hand on Nikolai's shoulder. "I have some of the finest vodka you will ever consume. Would you care to share a bottle with me, yes?"

"William," Elizabeth says disapprovingly.

Nikolai looks at him. "Is she some kind of saint?" He takes a hold of Elizabeth's hand. "Someone witnessed what you have simply confirmed. However, your honesty is appreciated. And do not worry. In bringing to justice, it is not you that I am interested in."

CHAPTER 12

Gavin looks at his face reflected in the mirror. "She didn't have a chance." He picks up his razor and begins to shave away the day's growth. "After all, I am a…superhero." He puffs out his chest and smiles widely. He begins to whistle, composing a tune. "Hey, that is not bad," he says, looking down into the sink, polluted with shaven whiskers. "I really should have a theme song." He leans farther into the mirror, his face taking up most of the reflection. "After all, I am…a superhero!"

Once dressed, he hurries down the steps, grabbing the keys to his car as he goes out the door. He was looking forward to dinner with Brig and the drive they had planned that would follow afterwards.

A half an hour later, on the tree-lined street of Brig's hometown, Gavin puts a few quarters into the meter for his car as Brig walks ahead of him. He pauses, for a moment, distracted by Brig's stroll down the sidewalk. She moved the way a woman should. It did seem schooled, however, as if it had not come naturally, but he did not hold this against her. In fact, he appreciated the effort.

On their very first date, they had gone whitewater rafting. She had proclaimed to everyone, "I'll do anything once," and then whispered privately to him, "It's the second time in doing something that's more difficult." It was this, her sense of adventure, coupled with her honesty that made Brig so appealing. But Gavin knew he was just kidding himself about admiring Brig's personality. There was really only one reason why he wanted to date Brig.

"The food here is wonderful." Brig places her chin on Gavin's chest and then swings around, leading him into the restaurant that she had recommended.

"You're a big eater, aren't you?" Gavin jokes.

"I'm not shy about what I like."

Gavin scratches at his face and grins.

Inside, the aroma of steak and seafood permeates the air. There is a large party jammed into the waiting area. Brig makes her way through the crowd to put her last name in for a table. Gavin finds a corner to hide in. When Brig returns, Gavin takes her hand and pulls her in close.

The large party is taken to their table, and Gavin can finally see the rest of the restaurant. As the hostess calls Brig's name, Gavin notices a familiar figure at the bar.

He hesitates, "Brig, you take the table. I'll be right over. I see someone I should say hello to."

Walking up to the bar, Gavin pulls out a stool, "Faulkner?"

"Gavin!" The professor says a little louder than he needed to. "How are you?" he asks, forgoing to adjust his volume.

"You're a bit buzzed," Gavin states, almost missing the seat of the barstool.

"Yes, Gavin, I know. I've done it enough times to know that I am."

"O…kay. When did this start?"

"Oh…" Professor Brickley lifts the glass that he had been clutching. He swallows the contents in one gulp. "Right after Emily died." He laughs faintly. "Isn't that ridiculous? A professor of Theology and I turn to this."

"You should have told me. I could have helped you. I could have at least referred you to someone."

"Please, Gavin, I might have lost some self-control, but I haven't lost my mind. I still know better than you." Professor Brickley retrieves his glass again. Now empty, he motions to the bartender. "I should have seen it coming though, being that my father was an alcoholic."

He points to the table near the window for the bartender to see that his intention is to move. "Let's take this meeting to a more formal setting," he says to Gavin as he folds the newspaper he had been reading under his arm. He groans as he gets up.

"Actually, I'm here with someone."

"Oh?"

"Yes, she's right over there." Gavin points at Brig, and she motions for him to come to the table.

"Ah, she's very beautiful, Gavin."

Professor Brickley takes the seat at the table near the front window. A cup of coffee is waiting for him there. He slaps his newspaper down on the seat beside him and shoots a frown in the direction of the bartender. He rests his arms on the table around his cup of coffee. "I loved Emily at 18 when she hadn't a clue of what to do with her life. I loved her at 30 when she became content with me and married life. I even loved her at 40 when she got that crazy idea to travel to India."

Professor Brickley takes a drink of his coffee. A sour look comes across his face. "Single men have this fear that they'll be stuck with the same woman for the rest of their lives after marriage, but I tell you that a woman will change a thousand times."

"I have to get back," Gavin interrupts, thumping his hand against the chair.

"I guess you're the big celebrity now," Professor Brickley states, disregarding Gavin's attempt to leave.

"What?"

"I don't often get the chance to read the paper, Gavin, but I did catch the story about your leap into Brown Water Creek." Professor Brickley pauses. "And then there's that rumor floating around town that someone played chicken with a locomotive."

Gavin leans forward and whispers, "Yeah and next week, I'm planning to go to Area 51 to see if there really are aliens."

"You think this is some kind of joke, Gavin? You think you can abuse this gift?" Professor Brickley pounds his fist onto the table and scoots forward in his chair, readying himself for a fight, but then he pauses and slouches back in his chair. "God has quite the sense of humor, doesn't He? I can see it now, you standing out on the edge of that bridge, feeling...what's the word...ah yes, feeling as if you were indestructible."

Gavin straightens his posture and looks away.

"Yes, and then your cords break, and you crash into the rocks below. Brilliant, just brilliant." Professor Brickley waves his cup into the air. "You were being taught a lesson, Gavin."

"No, there was no lesson, because there is no God. Face it; I can do anything I want."

"Oh really?" Professor Brickley asks, taking the newspaper off the seat next to him. He unfolds it and pushes it across the table to Gavin. "Elizabeth has been shot."

Gavin drops down into the seat. He grabs at the paper and reads the bolded headline of the article that has been circled in red, "Local Resident Injured during Missionary Trip."

"Why didn't you tell me that she was the aunt of the boy who you saw get killed?"

Gavin moves his hand to his forehead. His temple begins to pound.

"Gavin, I do believe you're being rude to me," Brig announces, coming up behind him. She moves her hand up his back to his shoulder.

"I'm sorry," Gavin says, sliding the paper to the side. "This is Professor Faulkner Brickley, an old friend of mine."

"It's nice to meet you, Professor Brickley." Brig offers her hand. "If you don't mind, I'd like to retrieve my date."

"Of course." Professor Brickley grins at Gavin.

"Brig, can you excuse me for a moment? I just need to use the restroom." Gavin moves from the table and makes his way back a long corridor. He slams his arm into the restroom door causing it to bang into the inside wall. He turns on the water at the sink. He allows a puddle to accumulate in his hand and splashes it on his face. The droplets slide down his neck as he looks toward the door. He then stares at himself in the mirror.

"Since you're an old friend of his," Brig says to Professor Brickley still at his table, "maybe you can tell me, if he is upset."

"I can assure you that he is."

"Is it because he doesn't enjoy my company?" Brig questions with a smile.

"No, I don't think it's that. You're much too beautiful. It's just that he's found out that someone whom he cares about has been hurt."

"Oh, I hope it's nothing serious."

"It's serious, but I think she will pull through." Professor Brickley takes another drink of coffee, sits it back into its saucer, and pushes it to the center of the table. "However, I'm not sure that he will be able to pull through."

"Why? Is this person a secret love?" Brig asks teasingly.

"Yes, she is."

Gavin maneuvers quickly through the tight rows formed by the tables in the dining area with his attention on Brig. She is looking around as if she were uncomfortable.

"I think I should go," she announces as he approaches.

"Why?" Gavin glides his finger around the inside of his shirt collar, which has gotten wet from the water at the sink.

"Professor Brickley filled me in on what is going on." Brig glances at the professor and then utters under her breathe, "Maybe we should do this another time."

"No, really, it's nothing," Gavin counters.

"No, I think we both know…it's something." Brig pats her hand on Gavin's chest and then walks to the door.

"Don't worry, Brig, you could have never replaced her," Professor Brickley says as Gavin follows her to the door.

Gavin stops and turns around. "What?"

"Let Brig go."

"I don't think so," Gavin says, exiting the restaurant.

Outside, he surveys the street, but he does not find Brig. Professor Brickley's meddling. The old man had always wanted him and Elizabeth to be together, but now there was an added incentive: Send Gavin to where Elizabeth was, and when he sees the shear inhumanity of the place, it will change him for the better.

He decides to walk in the direction of Brig's house in hopes of finding her on the way. A street light flickers as he passes by. The evening is calm as if after a day of battling the remnants of summer's humidity, the coolness of fall had finally won out. His hands turn cold as he progresses. He curls them into fists and pulls them up into his sleeves. With his shirt still damp, he flips up the collar of his suit jacket and draws up his shoulders. He lets out a long exhale.

The news of Elizabeth's injury had, of course, caused unanticipated feelings. He takes a moment to wade through them, analyzing their possible consequences. He realizes that he had one thing yet to fear: ending up like Professor Brickley, drooling over a glass of liquor. Each thought occupied by a memory of a woman. He pauses and then turns, starting another journey in the opposite direction, toward his car.

CHAPTER 13

Running his hand along the rusty rail, Gavin ascends the steps of the porch. He feels his strength returning for what he is about to offer to do. He rings the door bell and hears someone running toward the door.

"Mr. Bahn." Thomas says, attempting to open the door. A throw rug at the foot of the door lumps into several pleats, impeding his efforts. "This stupid new mat doesn't work here," Thomas grumbles like an old man, continuing to fight with the carpet.

"Are your grandparents at home?" Gavin asks through the small opening of the door that Thomas has managed to create.

Thomas tugs violently on the door. "My grandparents are out back packing some things for Aunt Elizabeth and the other volunteers." Thomas pushes his hair off his forehead and sighs loudly as if his battle with the door and rug has exhausted him. "You're here because of Aunt Elizabeth, aren't you?" Thomas begins again to pull on the door.

"I see you haven't changed, Thomas. Still getting right to the point."

"My advanced classes at school help me with that."

"Ah."

A moment's pause.

"You're going to try and get Aunt Elizabeth to come back, aren't you?" Thomas asks.

"I am going to see if she is all right."

"Yeah, but you're going to try to convince her to come back."

"Maybe."

"You can't do that. She still has work to do there." Thomas begins again with the door.

"I will be bringing her back, Thomas, and I'll lock her in a closet once she's back if I have to. Here move off the rug." Gavin loosens the carpet from under the door. In a huff, Thomas sends it to the middle of the room.

"Gavin?" Bea says, appearing at the door. "I guess you're here about Elizabeth?"

"Yes."

"He's hoping to bring Aunt Elizabeth back, but he can't do that, Grandma."

"Thomas, go and finish your homework."

"Grandma!"

"Thomas."

In defeat, Thomas begins to walk away.

"Why on earth is the rug in the middle of the floor?" Bea asks. At this, Thomas picks up his pace and disappears down the hall.

"I'm sorry, Gavin. Would you like to come in?" Bea inquires, turning her attention to him.

"No, Bea. Thanks."

"I suppose Juan talked with you?" Bea asks.

"Juan? No."

"Oh, he didn't? Well, a day or two ago when we got the news about Elizabeth, he called and offered to go over and see her. He said he felt responsible for encouraging her to go. I told him that she had the idea of going long before he put it there." Bea's face soars. "I thought for sure her travel phobia would put an end to the crazy idea. We've just been a mess since it all happened, and as you can see, Thomas has himself all worked up. So Juan didn't call you? He told me he would. He wanted to ask if you'd want to go with."

"I haven't spoken with Juan about it."

"But you are going to see Elizabeth like Thomas said?"

"Yes."

"Oh, Gavin that's wonderful! Her father and I have been worried sick. You're a Godsend."

"Yes."

⅄

The airport's asymmetrical glass and steel roof seem to carry out a greater purpose than just merely flooding the room with light. To Gavin, it was as if the architect had wanted to create an atmosphere where travelers would get a taste of the unfamiliar, foreign place that they were about to journey to.

Gavin stands holding a box full of cocoa powder and some other non-perishable items. Getting annoyed with its weight and awkwardness, he lets it drop to the floor. The thump echoes into the space.

"What's with the box?" Professor Brickley asks, sluggishly approaching Gavin.

"Her parents asked me to deliver it to Elizabeth and the other volunteers."

"I was wondering about it in the car, but you seemed a bit cranky this morning, so I didn't ask." The professor massages his left arm as if he were the one who had been carrying the box.

"Yeah, well, thanks again for driving me here this morning."

The professor gives Gavin a smile. However, the expression erodes away, as an announcement comes over the intercom system. "Something…" the professor pauses.

"What?"

"Nothing, nothing, now let's get you on that plane, shall we?"

"Yeah, will you be able to find your way out of here?"

"Yes, yes, don't worry about me."

"Okay, well I guess…you got what you wanted."

"Yes, yes, lucky me, always getting what I want." The professor picks up the box, hands it to Gavin, and pushes him in the direction that he should go. "I'd say, stay safe, but we both know there's no reason for that."

"Okay, are you sure you're all right, Professor Brickley?"

"Yes, Gavin now go before you miss your flight."

"Yeah, okay," Gavin says, contemplating whether or not to believe the professor. Twice he looks back as he walks away, just to make sure.

The professor remains in place until Gavin is too entangled in the crowd to see him. He then scampers toward the airport bar.

"Scotch," the professor says, ordering from the bar. He fumbles with the barstool. He looks to his right and then to his left as if he were expecting someone to jump out at him. The tingling in his left arm becomes difficult to ignore. He lowers his drink, beginning to feel a stabbing pain in his chest. Sweat forms on his brow and nausea overcomes him. Adding up the sums, he comes up with a total. "Bartender, get me an ambulance."

"Sir, I'm sort of new at this job," the bartender confesses, continuing to wipe down the bar. "I'm not familiar with that drink. What's in it?"

"No, you misunderstood." The professor grabs at his chest. "Call 911."

Gavin's view from the window of the plane turns from green and brown land to bright white clouds. Despite his fear of heights, as a young boy, he had always been fascinated with the idea of flying, but ever since the death of his father, his wonder had turned to mistrust. Now, like most everything else, he hadn't a fear about it, but he did consider the possibilities.

"Where are you heading?" the man next to him asks.

Gavin keeps his view out the window. "A refugee camp in Russia."

"The Chechen wars, right?"

Gavin nods.

"Boy, those Russians sure messed that capital up." The man begins to laugh but is interrupted by a coughing fit that lasts longer than Gavin would have expected. The man places a handkerchief over his mouth as his cough begins to calm. "So I guess this isn't a vacation."

Gavin glances at him and sees that the man's face has turned red from coughing. "No, I'm going to see a friend."

"She must be something." The man grins and slips on a pair of headphones, unplugging himself from his surroundings.

Gavin ignores the comment, leans back against his headrest, and closes his eyes. He replays the morning scene with Professor Brickley. When it came to the professor, weird was an expected trait. Rubbing his forehead and opening his eyes, he concludes that the professor must have been due for another drink.

Gavin yanks the airline's magazine out of the seat pocket. Paging through, he notices the issue is about the airline's attempt at volunteerism. A picture of a pilot in a bleached white shirt smiles with bleached white teeth. He stands in a mass of children precisely half his size. He looks awkward, out of place, as if he had chosen the shortest straw and won the prize of being the host for the day.

Another picture, a close-up of a woman hugging a child on either side of her, does a better job of showcasing the airline's attempt. The woman looked so comfortable with the youngsters that it seemed as if she would have rather worked in a school than in a large impersonal airline terminal.

Gavin slides the magazine back into the pocket. He wouldn't have been surprised to learn that the next day the woman had handed in her resignation in order to pursue a career in teaching or something along those lines.

He too had once resigned from a former life after recognizing that it no longer fit. He had even given Elizabeth notice, handing it to her bluntly, and creating a separation that had lasted for years before a chain of events had brought them back together again.

"Coincidence," she had said to him after the funeral. That was, of course, his explanation for the chain of events. It was likely that the modern dictionary was full of such words, words that ate at the very idea of God or all together canceled Him out of existence. Words that, before the modern age, probably never existed. In those days, the reason given for pattern in a chaotic world was always, G-O-D.

⅄

Nearly eight hours later, Gavin steps out of a cab, arriving at the doorstep of Harrison Spenser, a retired missionary and long time friend of Gavin's father. After a night's stay at Harrison's, Gavin was to continue farther east than he had ever traveled before.

After several quick knocks, a woman opens the door, instructing him to part with his belongings. He follows her down a hall to a room on the right. She points into the space. "You'll find the master in there, dear."

A Great Dane strolls by. He sniffs Gavin briefly and then hurries up the stairs as if he were late for an appointment.

Gavin finds Harrison nestled into a chair near a vigorous fire; a book and eye glasses rest on his lap. After years of teaching in foreign countries and dealing with the constant changes to schedules, meals, and customs, Gavin wonders if this was what the old man had wanted—retiring to a life of habit where even the dog seemed to have the routine down.

Harrison shifts in his chair, revealing the cover of the book on his lap. *How to Treat Women* was an unexpected title.

Gavin decides to remain where he is, hesitant to jar a man of Harrison's years out of sleep. He scans the room. It is boxed in with shelves filled with books. A vase of fresh flowers, probably placed on the table by the woman who had greeted him at the door, looked out of place in the dusty masculine room.

"You can wake him if you like. He won't bite. It's only Thursday," the woman explains peeking in through the doorway.

"Okay, I wasn't sure if I should," Gavin says, laying his black coat down on the couch.

"And you are?"

"Oh! I'm sorry, dear. I guess I didn't say. I'm Rita. I'm with the church." She straightens the flowers in the vase and then wipes the dust off the table with her rag. "A few of us ladies help out the older members of the congregation. I'm just here to do some cooking and some hoovering." She rings the dust rag and casts a glare at the sleeping elder. "Harrison," the woman screeches as if she had been married to him for forty years. She then strolls away down the hall.

"Wha....what?" Harrison awakens slightly, shaken by the sudden burst of noise. His gaze drops to his lap, and he grabs for his glasses. Placing the eyewear on the bridge of his nose, he looks up. "Gavin?" He begins to get up and sees the cover of the book in his lap.

"What's this?" Harrison skips his hand over his nearly bald head. "Rita!"

Music explodes from the kitchen and then is silenced.

"Do you think she is in pursuit of me, Gavin?"

"It's a possibility."

"What use do I have for a woman at my age?" He opens the book, revealing a soft covered book inside. He shows it to Gavin. "Oh good, it even comes with a study guide." Harrison shuts the book loudly, gets up and moves to one of the bookshelves. He separates two volumes on antique cars and guides the "How To" in between. "She'll never find it in here."

He strikes his bony finger into the air, "Let's show you to your room. It's nearly nine-thirty, and as you know, your cab will be arriving here very early."

He leads Gavin up the stairs, showing him the bathroom and the room where he will be staying. He then bids him goodnight.

Gavin enters the guest room, sits his suitcase and the care package down, and begins to pull out his clothes for the next day. Laying his shirt and pants on the bed, he hears the closing of the front door and then a clicking off of a light in the adjacent room. The house quickly fills with determined silence.

Still on U.S. time and not yet tired, Gavin sits down on the bed. A loud creak punctures the quiet. Afraid of making another noise, he does not move. Instead, he surveys the pictures covering the wall in front of him.

The photographs appear to exhibit most of Harrison's life, from a skinny, young teenager to a plump, balding middle-aged man. In most of the snapshots, he is standing with a native or with a group of fellow workers holding a hammer, shovel, or Bible. The pictures illustrated the kind of life Gavin had once imagined for himself.

With his back beginning to ache, Gavin leans back on his elbows. The bed remains obediently silent. He searches for a picture of the elderly man that he had met downstairs. Curiously, he finds none. Perhaps, Harrison's desire to make memories had been replaced years ago by a reliance on memories already made.

Laying flat on the bed, with the scent of fabric detergent surrounding him, he stares up at the ceiling. Three large brown dots have stained the ceiling.

Gavin realizes that his life was very similar to Harrison's present existence. He could understand how others might find this troubling, but Gavin, who could probably expect to enjoy a longer life than the average person, could waste another ten years if he wanted.

At 5:30 AM, with the lights still off in the house, Gavin moves his belongings down the stairs to the door. He pulls back one of the tightly hung shears on the window to check for his cab. Not seeing it, he turns his head toward the steps.

"So you're on your way," Harrison says as he moves cautiously down the stairs with heavy feet, gripping the railing with each step; his Great Dane trailing behind him.

The dog maneuvers around Harrison and glares up at Gavin as if to say that he was in his way. Gavin slides his foot from the animal's path and watches as the dog strolls down the hall to the kitchen, where Gavin figures he would start with coffee and finish with reading the morning paper.

"I never thought I would end up like this," Harrison explains, stopping on the last step. "I have a house, a nurse, a maid and a dog. All the comforts anyone could require but I am absolutely miserable." He stumps down onto the floor and lets out a groan. "I have helped people all over the world, but now I'm of no use. I've become the one who needs the help."

Hearing a car out front, he points to the front of the house, and Gavin pushes the curtain aside again to see if it his cab. Gavin shakes his head in the negative. Harrison nods. "Cancer they said. That was a shock. I thought I would die a martyr, strung up in some hell-on-earth village. But I suppose it is true what they say…it's the things you never consider that get you in the end."

Gavin hears another car out front and sees a black cab at the curb. "I got to go. Thank you for everything."

"Of course, of course." Harrison grabs for Gavin's hand, shakes it, and then pulls him in closer. "You miss your Father, don't you?"

"Yes, he was a good man."

"No, no, I mean your heavenly Father." Harrison swirls his finger around in front of him. "I see it in your spirit."

Gavin lets out an uneasy laugh as he releases himself from Harrison's hold. He gathers his possessions together, deciding not to answer. He exits the house after a polite farewell.

As the cab pulls into traffic, Gavin lays his head back and closes his eyes. A worn-out phrase comes to mind that is slightly altered to fit the situation: "You can take the missionary out of the field, but you can't take the mission out of the man." Gavin concludes that for Harrison, at least, even cancer could not do that.

CHAPTER 14

Sunlight fills the internal space of the building with a kind of pale yellow haze. Elizabeth steadies her focus on the dust particles dancing around in front of her. They twirl into a spiral as she exhales.

William lifts the bandage on her leg as no words pass between them.

"You are healing nicely," William finally states.

Elizabeth wipes her palm across her cheek, dispelling a stream of tears. "Still hurts."

William pulls the old bandage off and replaces it with a new one, a job that was usually left for a nurse, but ever since the injury, William had seen to these small duties. "I enjoy seeing you in tears. You are more human, less saint-like."

Elizabeth snorts a laugh and straightens herself up in bed upon seeing Lindsey rushing into the room. "What's wrong?"

"Oh we're all cookin' up a storm in Zara's tent," she explains, rummaging through the box of pans near the heater-stove. "Zara wanted to show us some traditional recipes, but to tell you the truth, there's just too many of us. Well, maybe just one too many of us. Maria thinks she's now some kind of head chef, demanding this and demanding that."

"Lindsey!" Maria shouts from outside.

Lindsey snatches a pan. "Oh boy, gotta go."

William places his hand on Elizabeth's arm. "My friend Dyson assembled quite the team, yes? They help here and there, wherever they are needed. I have been impressed."

"I know. In fact, after Dyson's memorial, the team told me they were going on with the trip." Elizabeth explains and then pauses. "I was thinking of going along. Do you think I would be well enough to do that?"

William scrutinizes her. "If you choose." He then shakes his head. "You are either strong or stubborn. I am not sure which."

"Oh she's many things," someone declares from the doorway, "moral, smart, *and* stubborn—definitely stubborn."

"Gavin?" Elizabeth says, half believing her own words.

"He is friend of yours?" William asks, glancing at Elizabeth. The answer gets caught in Elizabeth's throat. "I see," William says.

Gavin keeps his eyes on her. "You hardly seem happy to see me, Elizabeth."

Again the English language seems to escape Elizabeth and Gavin turns to William who has extended his hand. "Dr. William Sweitzler."

Gavin offers his name and his hand.

Seeming to think he is intruding, William excuses himself from the room.

Gavin moves closer, regarding Elizabeth. To him, she seems to be in a state of shock but that was his doing. It was the other things that bothered him— things this place had done to her. A large bandage was covering the left side of her face. She had lost weight. Too much, he thinks. Dark circles color the skin under tired eyes. She looked weak, deflated.

"I hope for your sake that there really is a God because you have certainly gone out of your way to impress Him." Gavin says and then waits for an argued response. Not getting one, he points out a small window. "My father once said that the Russians would do everything they could to hang on to these republics in order to use them as a passage way to invade Israel in the 'Last Days.' It would be ironic if the Muslims were currently being an obstacle to that."

"Gavin," Elizabeth states, finally finding her voice, "I'm sure you didn't come all this way to discuss End Time prophecies."

"No. Hi," he answers cheerfully, taking the chair where William had been. He looks around and observes the simple structure. "You sure know how to pick a place."

"Gavin."

"Okay, apparently, I'm here to check on you. And I'm here to bring you this." Gavin rests his hand on top of the box that he had lugged halfway around the world. "You'll find in here cocoa, peanuts, and green beans. Yum."

"Gav—"

"And I'm here to tell you that your family misses you a great deal and that they want you to think about coming home."

"I was wondering when the cavalry would arrive."

"Well, I'm afraid it's just Juan and I."

"Juan?"

"Yeah, we traveled separately, but he'll be along later. He said he needed to visit a colleague in Chechnya." Gavin taps his thumb on the edge of the box. "Thomas was going to come, but the United States government thought him a bit too zealous for the region."

A laugh escapes Elizabeth. She could not believe it—Gavin here, in Russia, no less. She accepted his reason for why he had come. Probably her family and Juan had talked him into it. How they had done that was beyond her. She had to admit that it was good to see someone from home, even if the sight of that someone crumbled the fortitude that was helping to sustain her in such a place.

"It must not hurt that much if I got you to laugh. Mind if I take a look?"

Before she has a chance to refuse, Gavin folds back the hem of her long skirt. "Yikes," he taunts and then rests his hand on her leg. Looking up, he watches a blush come across her face and hears her breath catch. Grinning, he decides to break the tension, not wanting to lose sight of his goal. "And you're sure you weren't the one holding the gun?" He coughs a laugh and then looks down again at the bandage. He leans back in his chair and scratches at his unshaven face. "So what will it be, Elizabeth?"

Elizabeth turns her head so as to hide her eyes filling with tears. "I want to go home," she says, glad for the steadiness of her voice.

Chapter 15

At the entrance of the building, Gavin holds back a snicker seeing Juan in a bright orange down coat. The thing came close to the look and volume of a giant bowling ball. He then notices the weakness of his friend's handshake. "Hey, everything okay?"

"Yeah, I'm just a bit road weary from dodging all the landmines." Juan steps around his friend. "Miss Elizabeth."

Elizabeth hops up on one leg and embraces him. To Gavin, Juan seemed surprised, as if he were unprepared to see Elizabeth in such a state.

"I know," Gavin mouths.

"You didn't have to do this," Elizabeth says, feeling embarrassed. She points to a chair for Juan to take a seat.

"I blame myself for this. I shouldn't have helped you come here."

"I would have come with or without your help, Juan."

"You know," he says, looking over at Gavin, "that's pretty much what your mother said."

"Elizabeth?" Ovlur peers through the doorway, holding a soccer ball. Peeling off his shoes, he runs farther into the building. "We need a...ah, goalie on our side."

Juan turns to Elizabeth. "Don't tell me you've been playing soccer on that leg?"

"Of course not. I'm only the coach."

"Elizabeth..." Gavin utters in an angry tone.

She gives Gavin a goofy expression. "I'm kidding." She pulls herself up with one of her crutches and hobbles to the boy. "I'm still not up to it, Ovlur." She glances at Gavin. "But as I seem to remember it, Gavin, you once played soccer."

⋏

Elizabeth had some memory; Gavin had only mentioned in passing that he had once played soccer as a child. Now he huffed and puffed and nearly threw out his shoulder throwing the ball back into play. Of course, it mended quickly but that wasn't the point. The fact it had to mend at all made him feel ancient and watching the little balls of energy bursting across the dirt field didn't help either.

Elizabeth and Juan wave and laugh at him from the sidelines. Gavin decides then and there that he hated the place. It wasn't the region, which was actually quite striking with its mossy and ragged, Tolkien Middle-earth look about it, nor was it the people that he disliked, but it was the constant display of compassion that was required to keep a place like this going that made him nauseous.

Juan was partly to blame for Elizabeth's desire to come to this place and so was that grumpy Russian piano teacher from Elizabeth's childhood who had created a kind of fascination within her for Mother Russia.

From the sidelines, Elizabeth offers him a smile, an appreciative smile. Uncomfortable, Gavin casts his gaze again to the field, and he realizes that whatever had brought her to this region—early life experiences, a friend's interests, or her own caring personality—it was clear now that even she understood it was time to go. He would be glad to have her safe at home, even if once there, he would remain at a distance.

The ball is kicked out of bounds, and he glances over at Juan and Elizabeth again. This time, however, Juan is no longer laughing but has moved his attention farther down the field to Ovlur who has left the game to talk to some straggly looking man. Gavin figures the man was a relative giving advice on the game, but the expression on Juan's face seemed to suggest something more. Juan leans toward Elizabeth as if he is about to say something to her but is ignored as a group of women pass by seeming to inquire about how she is doing.

Gavin decides not to bring up the incident. He hoped that Juan would do the same. The last thing they needed was a cause for Elizabeth to latch on to that would prevent her from leaving.

William stands with his right arm outstretched over the cushioned part of one of Elizabeth's crutches. He flexes his arm, lifting his cigarette to his mouth. "We had a friendship for a short particular time," he says dryly. "You agree, Elizabeth, yes?" He relaxes his arm again over the crutch. "Prayers are said often, then occasionally said and then forgotten all together."

"I suppose all Christians are guilty of that from time to time," Elizabeth utters as she sits on the bed, pounding her fist into her bag of clothing to make room for her shoes. The effort drains her, and she pauses, putting her hand to her head where a bandage once had been. Recovering she continues, "But I doubt very much that I'll forget you, William. In fact, I think I'll make it my life's cause not to." She points at the crutch. "And I'm done with those."

"You are not."

"You can't make me use them."

Williams holds his hand up like a stop sign and smiles. "We should not argue until I give you something. I am sorry that I did not remember." He pulls out an envelope from his back pocket and hands it to her. "Dr. Reynolds asked me to give it to you the night her team left," he says, flipping it over as he passes it to her. "I dropped a little of the cocoa from your care package on the back."

"I'm glad you enjoyed it." She smiles widely and begins to open the envelope.

"Let's get out of this place, shall we?" Gavin says, coming through the doorway. He yanks the crutch away from William, causing him to drop his cigarette.

Elizabeth looks up from the envelope as Gavin begins to collect her other items together in a hurried manner. "Don't pack that, Gavin. I want to wear it," she instructs, getting a bit annoyed.

Flipping his lighter open, William flames another cigarette into life. He gives her an awkward hug. "I do not like to admit it to Him," he murmurs, pointing up to the ceiling, "but it would have been good to see you accomplish what you had set out to do."

"Well, you can pick up where she's left off," Gavin suggests as he retrieves Elizabeth's other crutch.

Elizabeth rubs her stomach. She wishes she were alone, but unfortunately, Gavin is right beside her. Thankfully, however, he is too busy unfolding a map to notice her discomfort. Unsure which way is up, he rotates the thing several times and then glances over at her with a frown. "Why do you do this to yourself?"

"What do you mean?"

"Your mother told me about your phobia."

"Ah, good old mom." Elizabeth takes a deep breath. "I guess I thought there was a reason to come here."

"What convinced you otherwise?" Gavin peers at her with his nose up in the air. "Was it the bullet to your head or the bullet to your leg?"

Elizabeth looks at her crutches that were up front, leaning against the seat. "It was the bullet to the leg that was the clincher."

"Well at least you didn't have to stay and be a witness in some trial," Gavin mumbles, as he smoothes the map out over his legs. He then runs his finger down the map in a jagged manner. Not wanting to be reminded of the distance, Elizabeth watches the driver position himself into the front seat, which after years of driving, had become an inverse image of his backside.

The engine starts, and she turns around. Looking pass the escort car, she watches as the camp grows more and more distant. Facing forward, she slides her cold hands into the square pockets of her winter jacket. A crumbling sound and the smoothness of paper alerts her attention to her right pocket. Pulling from it, she finds the envelope that William had given to her earlier. She had placed it there and then forgotten about it.

Gavin moves his attention from the map. "What's that?"

She ignores him and extracts the letter from its soiled holder. Unfolding the pages within, she begins to read.

Gavin watches as her eyes skim from line to line. He peers over her shoulder to glance at the contents, but she teasingly moves away. As she reads on, he does it again, just to be funny, but this time she seems to get more possessive about it, creating more space between them. "Oh great," she says, folding the paper in half.

"What?"

"I have to go back." She taps the driver on his shoulder. "We need to turn around." The driver strikes the steering wheel with the palm of his hand and snaps off a Russian word.

"Elizabeth, what are you doing?"

"Isn't it obvious?" Elizabeth taps the driver again. "Driver?"

Gavin crumbles the map in two, ignoring the crease lines. "Why?"

"You can go on to the airport, Gavin. I don't care, but I'm going back."

"Elizabeth, I did not come all this way not to bring you home."

She turns to him. "You know what, Gavin? You psychoanalyze other people all day long, but you want to know what I think? I think you came all this way just to get me back home where I'd be safe and sound for your own peace of mind."

"Yeah," Gavin responds, "and it turned out to be a lot easier than I thought." He grins and nonchalantly puts his attention out the window.

Elizabeth can feel heat moving across her face. "Driver, turn this car around!" she hollers and then christens him a new name.

Gavin turns his head so quick a slicing pain rockets through his neck. He grabs at it and stares at Elizabeth in astonishment.

The driver launches the car into a 180 degree turn—this time, without complaint.

CHAPTER 16

A light rain begins to fall, but Elizabeth does not care. Even after a bit of haggling, the officials would not let her back into the camp. "She will be here for only a short time and then go," William had argued on Elizabeth's behalf. The officials wouldn't hear of it. They were tightening access to the camps, so she, Juan and Gavin had ended up at the home of a local friend of a friend of Juan's. She would stay there until her team was ready to go.

The rain quickly tappers off, and Elizabeth hobbles out of the courtyard toward the center of town.

"Elizabeth," Juan yells from behind. He runs toward her making a spectacle of himself in his carrot-red down coat, which to Elizabeth made him look like a big orange bouncing basketball. "You better let me come with you. With those crutches, you're an easy target."

"Don't worry," she pats her coat under her arm, "I've got protection."

"What?"

Elizabeth opens her coat, revealing an aerosol gun inside. "I had a real gun, at one point, but they made me give it up."

Juan's mouth drops open a bit. "What?"

A SUV pulls in beside them next to the curb, distracting her from providing more detail. A skinny man jumps out and heads into one of the stores along the street.

Elizabeth glances into the vehicle and sees a child sitting in the back seat. She squints her eyes. "It's Ovlur." She says and then begins to wave at him. He glances at her and then quickly returns his attention to the man sitting in the driver's seat. Juan grabs Elizabeth's hand. His face goes pale as he looks at the driver.

"Do you know that man?" Elizabeth asks but does not wait for a response. She taps on the window of the vehicle. "Ovlur." He glances at her with a worried expression. "Ovlur," she says again this time knocking a little harder on the window. "Ovlur, I want you to get out of there."

The driver begins to holler something and gets out. Elizabeth pulls on the handle of the door and it opens. The driver circles around the vehicle, looks at Juan and elbows him. Returning the favor, Juan gives him a jab to the eye.

"Ovlur, get out of the car." Elizabeth instructs now leaning forward on the seat.

"No, Elizabeth," he utters and starts to cry.

In the corner of her eye, Elizabeth notices the other man exiting the store. He runs toward them. "Juan!" Elizabeth warns and then crawls into the SUV, grabbing for Ovlur's hand.

Elizabeth turns and sees Juan launching a few punches, but they result in nothing. He is knocked to the ground. Ovlur jerks his hand from her grip, jumps out of the other door, and runs down the street out of view. She hears the door behind her going shut. Wood cracks, and she sees that one of her crutches is in the way. The man grabs it and flings it out onto the sidewalk. It lands next to Juan who looks just about done. The man jumps into the SUV. She slithers to the other door, but the driver is already there. He shuts the door in her face. Complete terror overcomes her.

The man inside the SUV pulls her toward him by her collar. She swats at him. He laughs at her effort and slams her head into the window. The assault shocks her, and she halts her struggle.

The driver plops himself into the driver's seat. An angry conversation ensues between the two men.

A moment of inattention and Elizabeth pulls the aerosol gun from her coat. She turns, spraying the man who has her by the collar in the eye. "Ugh!" he yells and whips his hand to his face. She goes for the side door again, but it has been locked. She strikes the unlock button, but the window goes down. She hits another button. This time the door releases. She grasps the handle, only to hear the door lock. The driver laughs. She looks in the rear view mirror, and he gives her a perfectly white smile.

⟑

Gavin smacks his shot glass down on the wooden table. He submerges his chin deeper into his coat. He stares at the blackened wood in the fireplace. Tiny orange dots are all that remain of a once raging fire. He begins to pour another and misses, causing some of the drink to slosh onto the table. "Oops," he says like a mischievous boy and then downs the clear liquid. "Ah," he says, returning the glass to the table. "Apparently, my talent does little to protect me from the consequences of alcohol."

He offers the bottle to Juan. "Your friend apologized again and again about having to leave for work, but at least, he gave us his best vodka before he left." He slides a glass toward Juan. Juan's hands shake as he lifts the drink to his mouth. Gavin stares at him for a moment. "You look a little off this afternoon."

Juan points to the crumbled piece of paper on the table, "What's that?"

"Something I never anticipated," Gavin proclaims, knowing the history that had brought the sheet into existence and the outcome it had fashioned. He reads the first few lines to himself and then begins again out loud.

Dear Miss Kashner,

It is with great trepidation that I write to you, but I felt that it was for a purpose far greater than I, so I have given in to the demand placed on my heart.

We share a common association, although my link with this individual is familial in nature; your connection is based on a grievous situation. The tie I speak of is with my younger brother, Stephen Winters.

The moment I saw you, I recognized you from your picture in the newspaper article concerning your nephew's accident. I cannot express my sorrow at the passing of your nephew and greater still, on my side of it, the cause of how he died. As a doctor,

I see death every day, but never have I had to face the fact that someone's death origi-
nated, even though an accident, from the hand of someone I know and love.

With this said, I am still trying to come to terms with what has occurred, at-
tempting to find my own sense of forgiveness that I must someday give to my own
brother. Because of this struggle, I still cannot believe—and am amazed at—the
grace you showed him on the day he came seeking your forgiveness. For that, I truly
say thank you.

This world can be so evil, as we both know, and I had been surrounded, covered,
almost suffocated by it, but your one act of kindness broke through all that, reminding
me, allowing me to see, once again, God's nature.

Although it was through another troublesome occurrence, I know it was by no
mere chance that we met, for God wants to draw something good from this situation
too. That reason alone I feel that I must tell you, for I believe God is leading me to do
so, that God has a purpose for you here. Stay the course. Do not let the enemy win.
Although, you are broken in the physical sense, do not let it spread to your spirit. I
know that with His help you will find your way.

God bless you, Dr. Samantha Reynolds

"Who can resist a letter from God?" Gavin laughs and then lowers his tone. "Certainly, not our Elizabeth."

"Now I understand why she came back."

The buzz in Gavin's head keeps him from thinking on anything too serious, but one thought keeps bothering him: He was becoming just like Professor Brickley, a drunk troubled by a woman. Let down by his own efforts, he had hoped the alcohol would numb and dissolve his concern, but by the time he had gotten to the fifth shot, all it had done for him was make him feel silly and a bit hypocritical. "I'm worried for her, Juan, and I don't know why. These feelings—I don't know how to deal with them. I'm out of practice."

"I know things have gone bad, Gavin, but I'm afraid they're about to get worse."

Gavin's gaze slowly drifts over to Juan.

"I need your help."

"You need help to the toilet?" Gavin snickers.

"Elizabeth is gone."

"What?" Gavin pops his chin out of his jacket.

"I just tried to help her get Ovlur out of a van."

"What are you talking about?"

"They took her. I don't know where."

The situation takes a moment to soak into Gavin's vodka filled head. He lunges forward, grabbing a fist full of Juan's parka. "What do you mean they've taken her? Who took her?"

"It was that man at the soccer game. You saw him." Juan twists out of Gavin's hold and backs away. "I was going to talk to her about him, but I didn't want her to worry, so I talked to Ovlur directly. I told him to stay away from that man, but he didn't listen." Juan moves back toward Gavin. "I know you blame me for bringing Elizabeth to this place, but I think I can find her."

"How?"

"There may be someone who can set up a meeting with these men."

"Okay," Gavin states, turning away. "But what about in the meantime? Will they...hurt her before we can find her?"

"Hmm," Juan replies with his habitual response.

Gavin exits the home.

Juan races his hand to his eye. Gavin's sucker punch was quick but apparently not painless.

CHAPTER 17

Elizabeth rubs the back of her neck. Someone had struck her there—hard. Before her, is a man sitting on a wooden chair, his hair is shaven like that of a soldier, a white shirt and khaki pants are his uniform.

She senses someone positioned beside her. He nudges her shoulder with the end of his automatic rifle as if he wanted her to stand.

"No, no, the woman does not need to stand. We are not that traditional here," the man in front of her commands.

In Russian, something obscene about the Russian military has been carved into the wall behind him. Sofas and chairs, presumably once arranged in a neat orderly manner, stand scattered about the room. On the floor beside her, she finds a gray woolen blanket neatly folded. Her last remaining crutch is nowhere in sight.

The man in the chair smiles. "I apologize for the obscenity," he says drawing closer. His light brown eyes darkening as he does. Glancing back at the wall, he glares at the words and states with a tone of disappointment, "And for the misspelling."

"How dare you kidnap me," is all Elizabeth can think to say—like some aristocrat taken from her manor.

The man looks at her oddly. "You have not been kidnapped. You jumped into SUV."

Elizabeth considers this. There was some truth to the man's statement. She had taken one giant leap into their SUV. "But I was trying to save..." Elizabeth stops.

"Save?" the man asks sincerely. "Save Ovlur? From what? From his father?"

The revelation, obviously intended to bring fear, did just that. A pulse goes through Elizabeth as if someone had just pulled the lever for her nervous system. She begins to tremble.

Dasha leans forward and grabs the gray blanket that is beside her. He shakes it out. "We do not see many Americans around here," he says wrapping the blanket around her shoulders. "I am curious, why you are here."

"I'm a missionary," Elizabeth utters before thinking of the consequences.

"Well, missionary, you have placed yourself in the way of a long awaited reunion, but you have shown a great kindness to my son. You thought him in danger. This will not go unnoticed."

"Please, just let me go."

Dasha rubs at his chin and then stabs his hand into his jacket and pulls out her passport. He opens it, pages through, and reads from the last page, "Elizabeth, from Millerstown, Pennsylvania. How does it make you feel that I know where you live?"

Elizabeth's stomach tightens. "Please, I don't know where I am. I didn't see anything. I was unconscious."

"I cannot really know this, can I?" Dasha snaps Elizabeth's passport closed.

"What will you do with me?" Elizabeth asks through a throat that now felt as if it had been sewn together.

Dasha glances at the guard. "No one touches her." He then looks back at Elizabeth, "You may serve a use. We will see."

⅄

Gavin and Juan pass through the checkpoint at the border of the republic. A few more miles and Juan pulls the rental car off the road, parking behind the van of the person who supposedly would take them to the group who had kidnapped Elizabeth. A beast of a man emerges from the vehicle and without saying a word, throws a black hood at Gavin.

"Not your usual posh crowd is it, Juan?" Gavin walks toward the van foregoing to pick the hood off the ground. For his refusal, he receives two blows to the abdomen and one to the nose.

"Believe me, sir," Gavin says, still doubled over, "you'll never see me in this place again, so really, I don't need to wear that thing."

On the ground with his jacket and shirt flipped up, Gavin notices the circles of red marks, where knuckles had met flesh and bone, were restoring to the color of skin. For a brief moment, he falls into wonderment. The show ends with their host squeezing the hood over Gavin's head, smashing his sore nose in the process. "Thanks, I can tell you're not the mothering type."

Juan grabs hold of the hood. "Knock it off, Gavin." He pulls Gavin's face close. "This guy will kill me and try to kill you. He doesn't need a reason."

"He'd be doing me a favor," mumbles Gavin with a compressed mouth.

Juan clenches the hood more firmly, too tight for Gavin to catch a breath. He shakes his head in agreement, and Juan lets go.

The beast comes up behind Gavin, hoisting him to his feet. He twists his arms, roping them together behind his back. "GET IN VAN."

⅄

As the van drives away with Gavin in it, the sun begins to set. It colors a thick bar of sky in intense red as if someone had taken a scalpel to the atmosphere and cut it wide open. Juan turns from the view as a car pulls up behind him. A man leaps out of the passenger side and gallops toward him.

"Oh great, not these guys." Juan races to his car. Jumping into the rental, he slams the door closed.

The man smacks the window with the palms of his hands. He then leans in, pressing his nose against the window, giving Juan a scrunched smile.

Juan reaches over to lock the other door, but before he can, another man slides in, pressing a semi-automatic to Juan's temple.

"You have been missed, Dr. Gutierrez."

Juan raises both his hands.

"Dasha would like to see you too, but first Bulat is having trouble with his toe fungus again."

⼈

"WALK." The beast commands of Gavin after a short drive. Somehow the animal had gotten through several checkpoints with only the charm of his smile and the nod of his head despite the fact that he had an American jammed into his trunk.

The thug pushes Gavin forward. With no way to see or to balance himself, Gavin tumbles to the ground.

Put to his feet, he is forced to march at a steady pace, but the difficulty in walking blind soon becomes apparent. The oversized brute leading him isn't helping either. He freely allows Gavin to be hit by what seems like every other tree branch that overhangs the path. "Can you give me a little better guidance here?" Gavin protests, not able to help himself. "I know I'm a foreigner and everything, but I'm sure there are international standards that cover these sorts of things."

"WELCOME TO CHECHNYA." The creature laughs heartily and clamps down on Gavin's arm propelling him frontward. Gavin's shoulder absorbs most of the impact into what seems like the side of a brick wall.

"There you go again, misdirecting me," Gavin complains to the blank space in front of him, not knowing that his guide had circled back around him.

He is escorted up a few steps and hears the squeaking sound of door hinges. A musty smell hits his nostrils. A few more steps and a cluster of voices in the distance become audible. The voices grow faint as he is forced to continue onward.

"STOP." His host digs his thumb into Gavin's upper arm.

The scratching sound of a key being placed into a lock precedes one last final shove.

"I'll always cherish our time together," Gavin utters, attempting to conceal the apprehension he had about the whole affair. The beast lets out a grunt and slams the door closed as Gavin searches the walls of the room.

Chapter 18

Sitting tied to a chair in the middle of a nearly empty room, Gavin recovers from a beating by yet another fist that was apparently attached to a hyperactive punk on his eighth cup of coffee.

Initially, when the beating had begun, Gavin had assumed that the kid was doing it to prove his manhood or his allegiance to his leader, but as the youth energetically pounded into him with his bloodied knuckles, one after the other with an ever-present smirk on his face, Gavin began to understand that the kid simply enjoyed doing what he was doing.

Never try to keep up with someone who loves what they do. Gavin had thought of the quote, from his father after the thrashing had ended.

"Good morning," offers the man with a shaved head at the door, who Gavin had heard someone call Dasha. Arriving in the middle of the room, he lifts Gavin's chin with the tips of his colorless fingers. "It looks as if Nal has taken it easy on you."

"Yeah, I would consider getting rid of him. He seems to have lost his motivation." Gavin leans his head to the side and spits out the blood that had accumulated in his mouth. "See, hardly any result." He says this knowing that his face might be healing quickly, but his chest still felt as though it had been flattened by a truck.

"You Americans are all alike. Overconfident, even when you should not be." Dasha positions the only other chair in the room in front of Gavin. Taking a seat, he slides open Gavin's passport.

"What kind of business is it you do, Gavin?"

"Why does it matter?" he responds in between short breaths.

"I like to know who I am dealing with."

"I'm a counselor."

"Ah," Dasha responds, pointing with his thumb, "this could be useful here."

"I get that."

Dasha tilts his head to one side and offers a stern look.

"Where do you have Elizabeth?" Gavin demands as a smile fades from his face.

"Ah yes, the missionary who was…kidnapped. Do not concern yourself with her."

"You know she's why I'm here." Gavin grimaces as the pain surfaces in his chest and then finally recedes. "You took the money. You have what you wanted."

"I thank you for that, but it is merely down payment." Dasha straightens his back and leans away.

"Look," Gavin responds, "I know a lot of foreigners think Americans are all rich, but some of us aren't. We just have a lot of discount stores, where we can buy just about anything at rock bottom prices."

Dasha runs his hand across his shaven head. "You do know that your acquaintance with Juan is the only reason you have made it this far. He once helped me. I consider him a friend. Did you know that he was a friend?"

"No, he failed to mention that."

"I believe Juan is afraid of me, however."

"I wonder why."

Dasha's lips stretch like a red rubber band into a smile. "I like you, Gavin. You are arrogant but also courageous."

"Pardon me if the feelings aren't reciprocated. I normally don't go around making friends with terrorists."

Dasha bends forward. "I assure you Gavin; I am no terrorist. Terrorism only works on those who cannot take the sight of blood. That is why it will never work here." He grins, seeming delighted by his own joke.

"Still, some use it to benefit their pocketbooks."

"Yes, and some use it because they think it is a command of their faith, but I am a man of sensible faith. Allah does his work. I do mine. I do not mix the two, as some do. Are you a man of faith, Gavin?"

Gavin breathes in deeply. "No."

"Why? Did your God not do something you wanted?"

CHAPTER 19

The pain had hit suddenly and intensified, and the next place Professor Brickley had anticipated going was Heaven. Instead, he had ended up at the hospital.

"You've had a heart attack," a doctor had informed him without emotion. An angiogram was conducted, and a stent was inserted. The whole affair seemed to be just another day at the office for everyone involved. It certainly was not the dramatic end the professor had expected.

"I thought I was a goner," he tells the Dean who had stopped by his office to welcome him back.

His new student assistant, Sheila Trevor, gives him a questioning look. "You sound a bit disappointed."

"Well, don't call social services, Miss Trevor. I'm not suicidal."

"No, of course not. But we all have our problems, don't we?"

"Yes, I suppose so." He taps at the center of his chest. "But my physician says I'll be fine."

"In some ways," Sheila mumbles under her breath.

"Well, we're glad to have you back, Faulkner." The Dean shakes his hand. "I've got a mess of calls to make, so I'll leave you to it."

Professor Brickley turns to Sheila who has started writing something in her notebook. "Why is it I get the feeling you are trying to tell me something?"

Sheila fails to look up.

"Sheila, what's the matter?"

She shakes her head and then glances at him. "I'm just a little surprised is all."

"By what?" Professor Brickley straightens up in his chair.

"By *whom* would be the better way of putting it."

"You're being rather vague. What's going on?"

"My fiancé said he saw you out one night when he was with his friends."

"He should have said, hello." The professor suggests returning to grade a paper, his interest waning.

"I don't think you would have remembered if he had."

The professor stops what he is doing. "I see."

"He told me that you even needed someone to help you into a cab because you were so…"

"Okay. Okay. I get the picture." Professor Brickley raises his hand to his head. "I've disappointed you."

"Don't worry about me. You're the one with the problem."

"And welcome back, Sheila." Professor Brickley dumps his hands on the desk. He pauses. "You should know Sheila that the drinking…is well, something new for me. I wasn't really trying to hide it. I mostly just wanted to be alone with it."

Sheila raises an eyebrow. She wasn't buying it.

"And you know when I said I thought I was a goner?" Professor Brickley points out, wanting to change the subject. "Well, I really thought I was."

"Why?"

"I had a vision."

A smile breaks across Sheila's face. "I didn't know you were Pentecostal."

"Well, Sheila, God does supernatural things for us Evangelicals too, you know."

She laughs. "I'm sure He does. What was this vision about?"

"It was about a friend's…shall we say, talent, and how he would use it, and how I would meet my end." Professor Brickley explains and then goes into a bit more detail. "What I don't understand is why that part of the vision was incorrect—why I didn't die." Professor Brickley lifts his pen from the paper leaving behind a blot of ink.

"Hmm, maybe it wasn't incorrect. Maybe just how you interpreted it was wrong. After all, you did end up in the hospital."

"True, but why was I even shown that part?" Professor Brickley poses the question more for himself than for Sheila.

"You mean you don't know?"

"No, but I'm sure you're going to tell me."

"Hmm." Sheila places her hand on her hip. "Are you gonna listen?"

"Do I have a choice?"

"No," she says, giving him a stern look. "This situation reminds me of a story that my grandmother once told me when she thought that I was wasting my life away. She told me a tale about these two men. Both had an ambition to write a book, and one day, both got news from their doctors.

One was given the news that he was dying—the other was told that he would probably live to see his 90th birthday. My grandmother asked me which one I thought ended up writing his book."

Professor Brickley stares up at the ceiling. "I don't know. The guy who got the good report because he had more time."

"Urrrrr," Sheila sounds, imitating a buzzer on a game show. "No, the other guy, because his time was limited, and he knew he couldn't waste it or take it for granted. He got the job done."

"Clever."

"What I'm sayin' is maybe that piece of the vision was put there to motivate you to action."

"I like your analogy. I really do."

Sheila straightens her posture. "Well, thank you."

"But I really didn't need any extra motivation to share the vision with my friend."

Sheila slumps against the back of her chair. "Hmm, maybe it was more like a timeline thing—like this will happen after this happens."

"That's how I believe I should take it. I just got the one part wrong by mistaking having a heart attack with dying."

"Most people do." Sheila closes the notebook on her lap. "You know what would really be botherin' me about gettin' this vision thing partially wrong?

"What?"

Sheila hooks her pen onto the front of her notebook. "Wonderin' if I got the other part wrong."

Professor Brickley does not respond. The point was a troubling one, and one that he had not considered before because he had sent—no, he had pushed—Gavin off to probably one of the most dangerous parts of the world, thinking that if he encountered any resistance and was harmed, his gift would heal him as he went along, but now this idea was suspect.

"What you need is a Daniel to interpret your dream," Sheila proclaims.

"Know any?"

"I know a Daniel Forester, but he ain't ever understood…anything."

Chapter 20

In the course of a few weeks, they moved several times. It seemed someone would get word of a raid, and off they would go into the night, taking Elizabeth with them, often ending up at some place more dilapidated than the one they had just abandoned. The bombed-out building with three walls and a tarp for a roof was the worst by far. They only stayed there for one night. Apparently, even terrorists had standards.

The move this evening was quick and organized. It had not always been that way. Usually it was quick and chaotic, but either they were getting used to running or someone had hired Martha Stewart as a consultant.

As they drive from the half blown out warehouse where they had spent the last two nights, Elizabeth puts her hand to her stomach and then to her mouth. "I have to throw up," she says to the tall, thin man sitting next to her. He ignores her. "I have to throw up," she states once more. He looks at her this time, and possibly seeing the sickly expression on her face through the dimness, he yells something at the driver. Before the vehicle comes to a stop, he leaps out. She follows, leans over and does her thing. The man shakes his head and lights a cigarette. She does her thing again.

They drive for what seems like another few hours, and then the van comes to a stop. She is escorted into a farmhouse that appeared to be isolated from the rest of civilization and because of this, had completely avoided the wars.

An entire day seems to pass before she hears someone unlocking her door. She is told to stand, and she is led into a warm humid kitchen. "Clean dishes," orders a tall heavyset woman in choppy English.

At a small wooden table sits a young man. A semi-automatic rests at his finger tips as he slurps at his cup of coffee. Fresh flowers in a tin can have been placed in the middle of the table. The man timidly gestures at the native fall flowers and smiles at her. She wonders if there was something wrong with him.

She looks around, a bit bewildered. It was true that after Dasha's command she had never been treated violently again. At times, it even seemed as if her takers were novices in the world of crime and unsure as to what to do with her. However, she never expected this kind of freedom. She could only assume that this was the good that came from her attempt to help Ovlur. Why this "good" could not translate into just letting her go seemed to be found in Dasha's idea that she could, at some point, be of use to him. Exactly how this would come about both puzzled and frightened her.

"Clean dishes," snaps the cook, now at the stove.

Elizabeth obeys. She turns and slides her hands into the lukewarm water. She stares out the window as she scrubs away the grim on a big metal pot. The sun slips into the horizon and then melts like a broken orange yoke into white downy clouds.

Someone, she could not remember who, had once told her that the sun at this position was no longer the sun but merely a reflection of it. She begins to wonder if this were true. Fact or fiction, it seemed to be an analogy for what she was experiencing—that this was no longer her life but just a strange imitation of it.

But she did not want to live this counterfeit reality. She wanted her life back. At this thought, an unexpected strength pours into her, and it begins to stir an idea, a radical idea, an idea of escape within her.

Finishing, the guard points out the window to the lopsided outhouse at the back of the farmhouse. This was the worst part of being a hostage: the lack of bathroom privileges. With his hand on his sidearm he motions her to lead the way.

As they return from the outhouse a few minutes later, Elizabeth looks off into the inky black distance. The farmhouse sat on a knoll, secluded, surrounded by a grove of trees to its back and a row of hills to its left. She knew now that over the line of hills there was a village. She could not see it, but the evidence of its existence was in the columns of smoke that rose occasionally into the night sky.

She considered herself a good runner. She figured she could make it. Her leg was much better now. Besides, what would this guard do? He would not shoot her in the back. She was sure of that.

She sprints off. Glancing back, she sees the guard raising his gun. She ducks her head and takes a sharp right. No shots ring out; her conclusions prove true.

Over the crest of a single mound, she loses him and races down the hill in a straight line. The village becomes visible and disappoints. It is merely a collection of tents.

She hears the sound of running footsteps growing louder. The light from a flashlight illuminates her. She looks back again. A hand grabs her. She topples to the ground.

She flails her arms and legs, but his unexpected strength is too much. He yanks her to her feet. Retrieving his flashlight, he pulls her back the way they came, both inhaling and exhaling loudly as they go.

Back in her room, the guard locks her in. She throws a boot at the back of the door and lets out a scream. It was not her best moment, but she refused to give up. However, she realizes that there was one essential element that had been absent from her attempted escape.

Taking a seat on the cold cement floor, she remembers reading an article while waiting at her doctor's office. "What to do in a Hostage Situation" was the title of the piece. At the time, she had skipped over most of the article, thinking she would never find herself in such a circumstance. Despite this, the main point of the article had still sunk in: Get to know your captors. Dyson had suggested nearly the same thing, although for a greater purpose, when he had told them to build a relationship in order to witness.

She considers her guard. He seemed to be a miscast actor in a troupe of killers and hostage takers. To build a relationship with him could only serve to help so that when she ran again—he simply would not follow.

The ting of the metal basin being placed on the floor awakens Elizabeth. The cook grumbles something as she tries in vain to straighten her back. The cook then hobbles out the door, pass the guard, and back to her kitchen.

Using her fingers, Elizabeth combs her hair back behind her ears and digs into the cool water. She feels the guard watching and stops. She dabs her face with a rag. "What is your name?"

The guard fails to answer immediately as if he is registering the inquiry, contemplating whether or not the question was one in which he should answer. "I cannot tell you this," he finally states.

Elizabeth drops her hands to her lap. "What can I call you then? Do you have a nickname—something your family calls you?"

"My brother calls me Zhyogal."

Zhyogal says nothing more, and Elizabeth continues to dry her face and neck.

"You are American, right?" he whispers.

"Yes."

"I went to American university," he offers, glancing at the door.

Elizabeth is a bit shocked by this, that this man was in the United States, but she decides not to show it. "Which university?"

"I cannot tell you. Please stop asking me questions. You know I cannot answer them." He ends with a bit of a laugh.

"Zhyogal!" Dasha shouts from the doorway.

Zhyogal withers instantly. He turns away and abandons the room.

Elizabeth leans against the cold plastered wall. How Dasha's brother ever survived in such a place, she did not know. To her, he was the weakest link. This was not only evident by his submissive personality, but it was also apparent in how there had not been a consequence for her attempted escape. It was as if it never happened. In fact, her kitchen duty, which to her was more of a pleasure than a punishment, had just continued on as it had before the incident.

Possibly he did not blame her for trying to escape. Perhaps he thought better of her for trying. If this was the case, then her plan to build a relationship with him would work all the better.

CHAPTER 21

Gavin had been moved six times. Each time it was to a smaller room. This last move was to a closet that held a mop. Her name was Sally.

He is completely bored. This was the worst part of being a hostage: the monotony. He knew he had hit bottom when, on several occasions, he had attempted to psychoanalyze Sally. He surmised the mop was passive-aggressive with a severe case of bulimia.

Because of this boredom and being held in a room without windows, keeping track of time became a sort of hobby. He made estimations according to when his food was thrown at him and when he was hauled out to the outhouse. On the wall, he had begun to record the days by using a small stump of chalk that he had found on a shelf behind a bottle of bleach. By his count, he estimated he had been in the closet for one week and had been in captivity for three.

He wondered why it was taking his captors so long to decide what to do with them. He concluded sometime ago that their aim of getting a larger ransom for him and Elizabeth had fallen through because the go-between had been caught, injured, or killed, forcing them to orchestrate a new plan.

He wondered how Juan was making out. He had promised to go through other, more conventional channels in order to free Elizabeth. Gavin had told him not to bother since, as he explained, the Russians had a nasty habit of not distinguishing between the hostages and the hostage takers in their rescue attempts.

Gavin's own plans for escape were abundant. His strategies, however, were often ostentatious and relied more on plots from action movies than on any realistic tactics. That did not stop him from fashioning them, however.

One plan was to snatch a gun, take a man hostage and demand Elizabeth's release. However, in witnessing how the men treated each other around the place, Gavin could only conclude that a shot to the hostage's head would put an end to that approach.

As he saw it, his only true option was to build trust between him and his captors, and to convince them that he could be more valuable to them than money. It would be a struggle to do this because their relationship was presently not quite where it should be. He blamed himself for this since before his realization of his only true option, and still under the influence of the many comic books he had read during his lifetime, he had run—still tied to his chair—head first into a guard.

In the aftermath of this incident, which only served to leave him struggling on the floor like an overturned bug, they had handcuffed him to a stationary object and gave him a warning that if he attempted something like that again, he may not see tomorrow. Of course, he had snickered at this warning. However, this new development of being restrained had posed a new problem. Despite this setback, he planned to utilize the new obstacle to his benefit. A hefty metal pipe employed as a towel rack was the object he was attached to now, but in another hour, this impediment would become a means of illustration.

⋏

Gavin rubs his hands together to warm them. Again he tugs on the towel rack. As he jerks on the bar, the screws crawl from their burrows. Like a stubborn dog, one refuses, and he yanks on the bar again. It releases, and his elbow knocks over the bottle of bleach on the shelf behind him. The contents spill all over his arm. "Now, I'll make a clean break of it," he says to Sally as the fumes bite at his nose. As usual, Sally does not laugh.

After a few trial runs, he leans against the closet wall. The towel bar dangles from the chain between his handcuffs. The smell of disinfectant hangs in the air.

There is a rustling at the door. He guides the bar back into the wall. The door opens slowly. He gives Sally a wink.

The guard, the one who reminds him of Santa, moves toward him while searching his front pocket. Pulling out a coin, he slides his hand back into the pocket to continue the hunt.

The younger guard, standing at the entrance, yells something. He pinches his nose and gestures at the old man with his gun.

The chubby guard, finding the key, lifts it into the air like a found treasure. He laughs heartily and steps toward Gavin.

"See, he's got it," Gavin says loudly to the youngster at the door. He turns to the guard with the key. "Don't let him treat you like that. You're a better terrorist than he'll ever be."

The guard grumbles and places the key into the lock of the handcuffs, but before he has a chance to finish the job, Gavin yanks the bar from the wall and sends it into Santa's nose. Clause backs into the wall. He slides down its surface and spills out onto the floor like a bowl of jelly.

Gavin steals the gun from the back of Santa's pants and points it at the youngster. The kid does the same as he shouts a few phrases, nervously swaying back and forth. Gavin had not counted on this. "Come on kid! Pull the trigger," he yells.

He considers putting the gun to his own head, but like the incident with the locomotive, he couldn't quite bring himself to do this. Instead, he fires a shot at the youngster's feet. The loud blast from the gun disorients Gavin for a few seconds. But apparently the shot is all the kid needs, for the next thing Gavin feels is a hot line of lava ripping through his chest. He steps back into the shelves and then falls forward on top of Santa's back.

Less than a minute passes before the blackness fades and Gavin's mind begins to tune back into the world. He is lying across something large. His face is smashed up against the cement floor. He opens his eyes and blinks a few times.

He notices that Santa's gun is no longer in his grasp. He scans the floor and does not find it. He imagines the kid hurriedly swiping it from his hand, but why? Did the kid really think that under normal circumstances Gavin could have survived such an injury? Gavin had seen the broken circle of fabric right over his heart as he stepped back into the shelves of the closet. Initially, the kid might have been frightened about taking the shot, but evidently, after swallowing his fear, his aim was dead on.

Gavin begins to get up. This turns out to be a bad idea. Another ear-piercing blast and the kid nails him again, this time, in the left shoulder. The projectile breaks through bone, and Gavin grasps at the wound. The pain diminishes slightly, and then all at once, it evaporates. Gavin breathes in deeply as wetness leaks from his eyes. He covers his ears as the ringing in them intensifies and then fades away. Realizing that this torment could go on all day, he remains completely still.

From all of the commotion, a crowd forms at the entrance of the closet, and Dasha hunkers down beside Gavin. He glances up at the youngster who is trembling. Not knowing the real cause and probably assuming it was just another attempted escape, Dasha exhales in a tone of disappointment. He glides his hand across his squared off chin and looks at Gavin. "Americans," he complains and then directs two men to hoist Gavin down the hall.

The men escort Gavin into a room where he had initially been kept. He inspects the room as they enter. "Oh, the place of special memories," he proclaims out loud as the two men tie him to the small chair in the center of the room. "Nothing's changed, except that desk. That's new."

One of the men tightens the rope around Gavin's wrists causing Gavin to spurt out a bit of air. "Ouch!" he shrieks and then struggles a bit. "Haven't we done this routine before, boys?"

The men look at each other, apparently understanding, for they lift Gavin, chair and all, over to the large oak desk positioned at the front of the room. They elevate the loose top of the desk and then use a line of excess rope to tie the chair to the desk's side panel. "Good job, boys. I wasn't sure how you were going to manage that, but the loose top really made things go smoothly."

The man with the caterpillar eyebrows smacks Gavin's face with the back of his hand. The other man, the one with the octopus-like arms, laughs as he arranges a chair in front of Gavin.

After they leave, Gavin leans his head onto his shoulder. It was not the most comfortable of positions, but it would do. He closes his eyes. It was time for a nap.

Chapter 22

Gavin is so deep in sleep that he is not awakened by Dasha coming into the room. In front of Gavin's face, he places his closed hands. *Clap. Clap.*

Gavin jerks up. A long line of salvia drips from his mouth. He wipes his face dry on his shoulder as he straightens his back. "Oh man, that was a good nap," he says to Dasha as he takes a seat before him. "You were a seal in my dream, clapping on the shoreline while I dove into a crater of water."

Dasha does not respond. In fact, he appears a little unsure as to what to say. He looks Gavin over, stopping his assessment at the small circle of missing fabric on Gavin's shirt. "The young man has told me an incredible tale."

"Yes, well, I'd like to give you my version of events. I'll summarize it for you." Gavin inhales a chunk of air and begins, "I had been loosening the pipe in the closet for some time now. I apologize for not telling you this, but I had to keep it a secret, of course, because I was planning on using it to hit Father Christmas in the face.

"Now, once I carried out that part of the plan, I reached for the big guy's gun and fired a shot in front of, not *at*, mind you, junior who then amazingly, after a few moments of self-doubt, gained his composure and nailed me right in the heart.

"You should be very proud of your weapons' training program here, because I would be dead if it hadn't been for well, as a friend of mine believes, God healing me and bringing me back to life, which as you know is not a belief that I subscribe to, since I'm more prone to believe in the Evolutionary Theory to explain the whole affair."

Dasha leans forward. "Why have you gone to all this trouble? I know that Elizabeth is not your wife, but is she your fiancée?"

This time, it is Gavin who is unsure about what to say.

"Is she your...how do you say it in America...girlfriend?" Dasha reclines into his chair. "Have you ever even held hands with this woman?"

"Once, but I don't think that really counts since I was just trying to help her out of my car, but I know where you are going with these questions, and I was just going to tell you—" Gavin stops as a man in a shirt two sizes too big swings open the door.

The man strides into the room like a long-legged giraffe with beads of sweat trailing down the sides of his face, which was odd because it was freezing. He slowly walks over to Dasha while mopping up the perspiration from his forehead with a black handkerchief. He whispers something in Dasha's ear.

"Shoot him in right kneecap, and cut off right ear," Dasha answers while keeping his view on Gavin.

The sweating man then progresses back toward the door.

"Wait." The order stops the man's advancement to the exit.

"He can only hear out of his left ear?"

The sweating man dabs his face once more and answers in the affirmative.

"Then cut off left ear."

Dasha stands up and positions himself between Gavin and his chair.

"Was that for my benefit? Because really—"

The bullet penetrates just above Gavin's right eye, leaving behind a hole and a tributary of blood. Dasha observes his watch. The minute hand does not make a complete round before Gavin begins to stir. Gavin blinks a few times, attempting to focus his eyes. His neck muscles ache as if he had been forced to move in some unusual way. "What did you do?"

"I shot you in head."

Gavin groans loudly. He wasn't feeling any pain, but the idea of having his brain shot through made him queasy. The ill feeling leads him to a thought: How many of these deaths did he have to spare? The notion angers him because he had not considered this before.

"It was really the only way to know for sure," Dasha explains. He smiles and then presses his thumb against Gavin's forehead tilting it back. He then rounds his examination to the back of his skull.

"What are you doing?"

"I am looking for exit wound."

"There won't be one. It would have healed by now."

Dasha's eyes widen and then narrow to slits as creases of anger billow across his forehead.

"This is what I've been trying to tell you!" Gavin screams out of frustration and swears at him.

Possibly out of habit, Dasha lifts his gun again and directs it at Gavin.

"Wait. Hold on. I don't know how many of these lives I've got left. An infinite number or only nine and two have already been wasted on demonstration purposes alone."

Dasha steps back. "This has gotten very messy, Gavin. The boy that shot you will probably not shoot again. He thinks Allah is against him."

A gunshot goes off down the hall, and Dasha does not even turn in the direction of the sound. Gavin swallows hard, knowing that some guy probably just received a blow to his kneecap, with his screams more than likely obstructed by a single strip of duck tape.

"Usually when someone becomes a problem, I simply kill them," Dasha says, beginning to pace the floor. "But with you, I cannot do this. I should just drive you somewhere and throw you out of car or sell you to the Taliban. I hear they like Americans in their videos."

Gavin drops his head forward and sighs. "Do you remember telling me that you like to know who you are dealing with?"

"Yes."

"Well, I hope that I've demonstrated who you are dealing with, that I am someone you can trust to help you. After all, I could have just killed that guard." Gavin wipes away the trickle of blood that had made its way down to his chin. "But I will only help you if you let Elizabeth go."

Dasha begins to move away. "Gavin, your chivalry has impressed me."

CHAPTER 23

It is around a small wooden table that Dasha explains the events that have occupied his mind for the past few days. The words sound strange as he utters them out into the real world. He could not, however, avoid the telling of these events. For simple precautionary reasons, they had to be revealed. His younger brother stares at him in disbelief.

"The missionary, she is doing well?" Dasha asks simply to alter his brother's expression.

"Yes, brother," Zhyogal answers.

"I think you should talk to her more. Discuss her faith, maybe."

"Why, brother? She is a woman, and I thought you did not want me to talk to her. You said my manner caused her to think she could escape easily."

"I know, but don't you see? I understand these missionaries. They want to convert anyone who passes in front of them. She will want to convert you, I am sure. No, talk with her, Zhyogal, especially about religion. She will not want to leave you."

"I will, brother," Zhyogal replies, looking down at the table. He then lifts his head, "Are you going to meeting tomorrow with me?

"You go," Dasha answers. "It will be good that you take more of a headship role."

"I appreciate that, brother. These men, they seem to understand our anger."

"Or at least they know how to utilize it," Dasha says with a smile as he places his hand on his brother's arm.

There was a hint of something in the paleness of Zhyogal's skin and in the scowl of his features.

"You look as if you've seen a ghost," Elizabeth states, positioned at the kitchen sink.

"That would be close to truth," he says and then seems to want to say more but does not.

"I know, I know; you cannot say," she utters, scrubbing a pot that smelled like garlic.

The cook wrings a sponge over the sink and gives Elizabeth a frown, seeming to disapprove of the conversation.

Zhyogal turns to the guard who had been sitting in for him while he was out. A few words are exchanged, and the guard smashes his cigarette into the dainty flowery plate on the table. He rubs at his greasy nose and then disappears from the room.

Elizabeth dumps the pot on the counter and starts to dry it. When she finishes, Zhyogal escorts her back to her room after snatching a piece of golden-crusted, pumpkin filled pie from the counter.

At the entryway, he hands her the leftover food. She accepts it, taking in the scent of warm pumpkin.

Elizabeth bows her head to pray. When she is done, she glances at Zhyogal hovering at the door, glaring at her. "You pray before you eat?"

"Yes," Elizabeth answers.

She waits for him to say more, but instead he pulls the door closed.

Elizabeth waits for the cook to wash her knives for the second time. After drying them, she slides them into their fabric-lined drawer. Taking the key from around her neck that was attached to a dirty white string, she locks the drawer. Elizabeth was sure that this little obsession of the cook's about protecting her knives was not done on Elizabeth's account but was in place long before she had arrived.

At the kitchen table, Zhyogal is busy cleaning his automatic rifle, which is in pieces all over the table. After the cook scoots over to the stove, Elizabeth moves to the sink to wash two large spoons.

"You are a Christian missionary, are you not?" Zhyogal asks.

"Yes." Elizabeth pats the spoons dry as if to comfort them.

"When I was in America, I was given many books to read. One of these was the Bible." Zhyogal offers, causing Elizabeth to glance at the door.

"Do not worry about that man," Zhyogal explains, seeming to understand Elizabeth's apprehension. "Does it surprise you that I read this book?"

Elizabeth shrugs her shoulders.

Zhyogal grins slightly. "I must admit, even after reading it, I still did not believe that it was the Word of God."

"How do you know the Koran is?" Elizabeth pauses and then squeezes the dishtowel. That was a bad move.

Without answering, Zhyogal begins to reassemble his rifle. The pieces make a sharp click as he puts them back into place. The sound and quick movement of his hands make him appear upset. As he reconnects the final piece, he looks up at Elizabeth. "I could never understand how Christians could worship a God who was killed by mere men."

The statement seems to rid the atmosphere of something dark. "In battle, don't men sacrifice themselves to save other men?" Elizabeth asks, feeling her confidence returning.

"Of course. This happens."

"Well that is what Christ did. He allowed Himself to be sacrificed in order to save us, but unlike that soldier in battle, Christ did something that no mere man could have ever done. He conquered the power of death and sin in a single blow. Have you ever met anyone who accomplished that?"

Zhyogal does not say anything. He just sits there wiping down his automatic rifle. Elizabeth returns to her duties. When she finishes, Zhyogal walks her back to her quarters.

At the entryway, he hesitates to leave. He then steps into the room and leans his gun up against the inside wall. "I'd like to ask you another question."

Elizabeth looks passed him to the door. It is only for a moment that she allows herself to imagine that she is on the other side. "Go ahead, ask."

The morning's light fills the room, making the temperature in the space unusually warm. Was it the stuffiness of the room that had awakened him? No, there was a voice. He looks deeper into the sundrenched room.

The voice sounds again. This time, it calls his name. It was coming from somewhere farther in, where he could not see.

He was not one to take to fright. He had fought battles, seen things a man should not see, but he had never known fear as he did now. He begins to tremble as the voice calls again. This time a question is asked. Suddenly, on his right shoulder there is a touch, his body eases, and the question is asked again.

"You ask too much," he responds with a voice so raw he barely recognized it.

CHAPTER 24

Winter was settling in. Around her shoulders, Elizabeth pulls on a wool military blanket. She was cold now being away from the warmth of the kitchen. Zhyogal, with his sleeves rolled halfway up his arm, is situated near the door. It was a spot he seemed to have a habit of occupying.

"Zhyogal," Elizabeth says, "you've asked me a lot of questions over these last few weeks. Can I ask you one?"

He smiles weakly, seeming fatigued. "Yes, I would like this."

"How did you ever get involved with these men?"

He begins to roll down his left sleeve. "There were no jobs after the fighting had settled down, and I had to support my wife and child."

"Do they know what you do?"

"Yes, but we do not speak of it." He buttons his sleeve and then looks up. "What is it that you think I do?"

"Terrorism, gunrunning, et cetera, et cetera, et cetera."

"We are not terrorists."

"That's exactly what I'd expect a terrorist to say."

"We are not terrorists," he states, roughly brushing his other sleeve down his arm. "Although, there is place for such things. I believe you would disagree?"

"I abhor the idea that terrorist attacks are sacred events and that we should just sit back in awe and take."

He twists his wrist awkwardly in an attempt to fasten his right sleeve. "Many believe it is sacred."

"But you do not have to die to be accepted by God. Christ has already done that for you." Elizabeth points to his wrist. "Here, let me help you with that."

He becomes quiet but holds out his arm. "I must tell you," he says as Elizabeth tidies the end of his sleeve, "we will be moving again soon."

Elizabeth's stomach tightens. She sits back against the wall. "Not again."

As she utters this, she hears what sounds like someone tripping out in the hallway. Zhyogal goes to the door.

"Brother?" he says with a tone of puzzlement as he steps out into the hall.

"Ah, yes, Zhyogal," Elizabeth hears Dasha say. "I am here... to go with you to next meeting."

"But that is not until tomorrow," Zhyogal explains.

"Is it?" A moment's pause. "Ah, yes, of course, you are right. I do not know how I forgot these things. I will see you tomorrow, then."

Zhyogal lingers at the entrance for a few moments and then walks back into the room with a strange look on his face. "I think you will be needed in kitchen," he utters to Elizabeth.

⅄

The cook is off her game. Smoke fills the kitchen. Zhyogal lunges toward the window over the sink and yanks it open. He snatches a rag from the table and begins to fan the smoke to the outside. The cook grumbles something in one of the foggy corners. She points to her back.

"She says her back is not so good today."

Elizabeth waves the haze from her face. "Neither is her cooking."

Zhyogal chuckles as he makes his way to his usual spot. After a few more comments, accompanied with some hand gestures, the cook returns to mashing potatoes in a shallow bowl with a fork.

Elizabeth takes her place at the sink and recovers a serving plate from the bottom of the sudsy water. She rotates it in her hand, admiring the elaborate pattern that decorated its edge. The plate looked old and precious, like something swiped from a Tsars' dining table.

The cook barks a few words into the quiet atmosphere. Elizabeth jumps. The plate slips from her hands and cracks in two across the sink's divide.

Elizabeth holds her breath. The cook scrutinizes the fragmented plate with her hand pressed to her back. She raises her potato-coated fork and smacks it across Elizabeth's face.

Zhyogal charges forward and shoves the cook against the wall.

Elizabeth wipes the mess from her face as her cheek begins to throb. Zhyogal is yelling something. Smoke wafts around Elizabeth, up, and out the window. Elizabeth does not hesitate. She simply does what she has imagined doing a thousand times. She jumps onto the counter, maneuvers around the faucet, and escapes through the open window. Getting to her feet, she runs to the woods.

At the tree line, she slows her pace. In amongst the pines, she feels safer and more concealed. She takes a moment to catch her breath.

She is cold. She realizes she has left her coat back in the warm, dry kitchen. She will not last long without another layer of clothing. The need to cry rises within her, but she stamps it down.

She tells herself that Zhyogal will not follow, that her plan has worked. But this hopeful notion dissolves as she peers around the base of a tree. Zhyogal and the guard with the oily nose are about one hundred yards away.

She watches as the guard slings his rifle over his shoulder and proceeds onward nonchalantly, seeming more interested in taking in the scenery than in looking for her. Apparently, he thought this was going to be easy. And it would, if she did not think of something soon.

As the men move forward, she stays tight against the tree, circling as quietly as she can around it as they approach. She says a prayer that rounds itself back around only to be repeated once more, "Please don't let them find me; please don't let them find me."

Zhyogal stops twenty feet from her, and something crawls across Elizabeth's neck. She bites her lip. Zhyogal looks out ahead and then moves on.

Jumping away from the tree, she wildly brushes her shoulders and neck. Again, she wants to cry, but she refuses herself the pleasure.

In the opposite direction of the encampment of tents, she walks. After some distance, she settles down behind a fallen tree that has been taken over by moss and ferns that have yet to be hit by the winter frost. She waits for nightfall.

As the light fads, the forest evolves into another creature—a dark and unfriendly one. This was going to be creepier and more difficult than she had anticipated. Like a woman in an annoying horror movie, she trips over branches and falls into a hole. "Good grief," she mumbles to herself, "I used to be a Girl Scout." She rubs at her cheek where the cook had struck her. "However, I never had to run from Chechen Terrorists."

Pulling herself up out of yet another hole, she begins to pray. "How did I get myself into this, Lord? Oh, I remember; You wanted me to come here." She says, brushing her hands of dirt. "Just so You know, the next time You tell me to do something, I will think twice about listening. And You certainly could not blame me for doing so."

The rambling, complaining prayer ends when she reaches the edge of the woods where she finds the residents of the camp she had avoided during the day. Sitting around several campfires are numerous groups of men. Not a single woman is in sight. Defeat overcomes her, but then hanging across a tent line, she sees a jacket.

She blows into her hands and dashes to the line.

Seizing the coat, she sprints back into the trees, allowing the forest to envelope her. She turns to see if anyone has heard her. A man sitting at the fire glances in her direction. He gets up and scans the boundary of the woods. Elizabeth remains in place. He looks right at her. She holds her breath. Seemingly not to have actually seen her, he spins around and returns to the warmth of the fire.

Relieved, Elizabeth hunkers down, piling forest debris over her legs for the night. It would be a long one.

$$\lambda$$

Blackness fades to a hazy blue, and Elizabeth begins to stir. Something, however, is preventing her from moving very far. She looks down and sees an aggressive vine wrapped around her. She follows its long stems and begins to peel them one by one off her arms and legs. One strand is even resting on top of her head. Being cold, she must have drawn them over herself during the night.

Like a stiff, cold zombie, she stands from her forest bed. She looks toward the camp. The fires that were popular the night before have been abandoned and left to smolder. Her stomach grumbles.

It was true that the country's woodlands were full of edible items. Dasha had probably survived because of this when he had hid from the Russian military, but for Elizabeth, this was of no help. She could not distinguish between a winter berry that was edible or one that would kill her instantly.

Left to rely on the encampment, she creeps into the site. Through the ash of a burnt-out fire, she hunts. Nothing. She goes to the next ring of stones. Nothing. She sneaks deeper into the camp and farther away from her hiding place. A man snores in one of the tents next to the third campfire. A wooden skewer with a piece of burnt meat at the end rests across a rock near the fire. Like an animal, she snatches it and makes her way back to the trees.

Biting off a bit of the unidentifiable meat, she grieves for the cook's food, especially the siskels, the griddled corncakes that you dipped into a yogurt and cheese spread. Perhaps that was Zhyogal's plan. To let her starve in these woods until she came running back, begging for a plate of lamb stuffed dumplings.

Swallowing the last piece of the hardened meat, she wonders how these men and their supplies had gotten to this remote location. There must be vehicles somewhere.

Getting up, she begins to encircle the camp. There, nestled in amongst the trees, are several 4x4 trucks. She rushes to them.

She tries the door of one. It opens, but there are no keys. She starts to back away but then sees the keys on the floor.

Sliding into the driver's seat, she imagines herself careening down the mountain road, a road that would take her back to her family. She would hug Thomas so tight and not let go. He would hate every minute of it.

She begins to close the door, but something hinders her from completing the task. She glances up. Zhyogal's is standing outside the door, his hand on the handle. His face is unshaven, which made him look older, less innocent. "Elizabeth," he says to her as if she were his child.

Fear pulsates through her, but stubbornly she tugs on the door to close it. Zhyogal resists her efforts with his greater strength. Opening the door all the way, he plucks her from the vehicle. "I promise; you will not be hit again."

"Is that why you think I ran?" Elizabeth tries to struggle free. "Please, just let me go."

"Don't beg me, Elizabeth; you make me feel like a monster."

"You are a monster if you don't let me go."

Zhyogal's expression darkens at this.

Men begin to emerge from the tents, awakened by the commotion. Zhyogal says a few words to them, and they keep their distance. He then tightens his grip on Elizabeth's arm. "Your friend, Gavin, we have him." Possibly seeing the confusion in Elizabeth's face, he says it again.

"How did he find me?" Elizabeth finally asks with a worried tone.

Zhyogal stares at her for a moment. "You don't know about him. Do you?"

"What do you mean?"

Zhyogal looks away. "You must return with me, or he may not survive."

"I don't believe you. You wouldn't do that," Elizabeth utters.

"Do you really want to take that chance? I am monster, after all."

⅄

The gathering was taking place in an old bombed-out factory building where, on a daily basis, people from town had once made a simple living. The town and the people were no longer there, however. The Russians had destroyed them and it years ago. This history, distracts Dasha, causing him not to contribute to the discussion.

"Do you have anything to add, brother?" Zhyogal asks, seeming to notice his brother's distraction.

"No, Zhyogal," Dasha answers, standing from a table that seemed to be surrounded by every Islamist from here to Iran. "My brother is becoming quite the leader. Is he not?" Dasha utters, placing his hand on Zhyogal's shoulder. The group answers with general agreement and then returns to various conversations. Dasha walks outside to a loading dock that was still attached to the factory building.

Zhyogal observes his brother just as he secretly had two days ago when Ovlur had been returned to them. It was part of their Chechen culture not to show affection to their children in public, and Dasha had followed this as he greeted his son. But then alone, when Dasha thought everyone had gone, Zhyogal had viewed through a cracked door his brother embrace Ovlur with such tears and words of guilt that it bordered on desperation. Zhyogal had turned away at the sight of it, possibly because the display had illustrated a bond that he had never experienced.

Seeing that his brother was not returning to the table, Zhyogal excuses himself and goes over to him. "You should be thankful for these men," he says to Dasha, "they have returned Ovlur to you."

"Yes, I am very thankful for that," Dasha responds.

"I bought Ovlur something—a Koran," Zhyogal offers. "Just as my son is, Ovlur should be memorizing it—learning from it. You could provide Ovlur with something our father never did." Zhyogal then turns and points to the men at the table. "He could also learn much from these men."

Dasha does not respond.

"He should stay with Alma, in particular, for awhile and learn from him," Zhyogal continues. "He is a very wise man."

Dasha glances at the group of men, "Alma straps bombs to women and sends them out to do his bidding as he sits here in his finest suit."

"Well, someone must lead us," Zhyogal counters.

"I prefer to lead myself, Zhyogal. I may be a violent man, but I want something different for Ovlur."

"Forgive me brother," Zhyogal continues with some irritation, "but you do not seem to respect these men nor do you seem to care about what they can do for us. You do see that with their help we can finally carrying out the blow to Russia that we've desired all these years. We may even be able to send a message to the West."

"I am cautious, Zhyogal that is all. Age, has a tendency to do that."

Zhyogal rubs at his brow, "The American woman, she has tried to escape again."

"Oh?" Dasha responds.

"Yes," Zhyogal answers and then observes the group of men. "You once said that she could be of use to us. Giving her to them, could help us in this agreement."

"No," Dasha says sharply causing Zhyogal to raise an eyebrow. "No," he repeats this time more softly, "I have other use for her, Zhyogal. It is my own sort of revenge."

Zhyogal expression turns to one of confusion.

Chapter 25

Through a small, painted shut window in an upstairs room, Elizabeth surveys her narrow view of the landscape. The scene had become a kind of clock where she could observe the passing of time: the end of winter, the beginning of spring, and then early summer.

This newest location was a much larger farmhouse with indoor plumbing, which seemed to indicate that her captors had become more successful in their pursuits. Things had gotten better for them but not for her.

Lately, she had not been offered much to eat. That was the trend ever since the cook had taken a utensil to her face. The cook may have been one mean lady, but at least, she cared about seeing that everyone was fed. But the cook had made a mistake. She had disobeyed Dasha's order and that was what happened to people who did not listen to Dasha—they simply went away.

Elizabeth rests her head against the cool glass of the window. She closes her eyes, and her mind drifts to Justin. Even after all that had happened, the ache was still present from the loss.

The sound of giggling children makes her smile, but then she realizes that the laughter was not from a memory but was coming from out in the yard. She opens her eyes and sees a child running to a car that Dasha was standing alongside. "Ovlur." Elizabeth utters softly. She slams her hands against the wall surrounding the window. "Ovlur!" she shouts but to no avail. The car drives off without Ovlur noticing.

Elizabeth slides down into the corner of the room. The sense of defeat that she was experiencing, however, quickly turns to fear as she hears unfamiliar foreign voices just outside her room.

The door swings open, revealing a group of men gathered behind Zhyogal in the hallway. They peer at Elizabeth as if she were an animal on display at a zoo. Zhyogal looks at her without recognition. This, however, did not surprise her; something had changed in his manner toward her ever since the day she had called him a monster.

Outwardly something had changed as well. His beard was just about the right length now, which allowed him to fit in with the other men who were standing in the hallway.

One of these men turns and asks Zhyogal a question. He leads them away, forgoing to close the door.

Elizabeth stands and then pauses. The boy is barely 6 years old. From the doorway, he watches her with his familiar brown eyes—the same as Zhyogal's. He begins to recite the English alphabet, "A, B, C, D…" Finishing, he gallops to her. She is unsure what to do. Praising the child for his English seemed ridiculous. She decides not to pay him any attention and begins to approach the open door.

The boy trails her. He tugs at her pant leg. She ignores him. He tugs again, saying, "One, two, three…" he counts, grabbing one finger after another bending them back as he goes. Elizabeth smiles, nods, and then continues on her way. The boy then smacks her leg hard with his open hand.

"What?" she cries.

He moves his tiny hands into the shape of a triangle. "Look at the church. Look at the steep-le. Look inside at all the dead—"

"Dakka," a woman yells from the hallway and motions for the boy to come to her. The boy seems to panic and remains behind Elizabeth. For a moment, the woman studies Elizabeth, seeming to look at her with pity, but then she shouts again. The boy scurries to his mother's side but not before one last curious look at Elizabeth.

Gavin leans forward on an ornately carved chest of drawers. He stares at a tapestry hanging behind the antique cabinet. His eyes follow the woven threads of the border as people begin to take form within the geometric shapes. He reaches out his hand and touches the figure of one of the people being led along by a threaded word of calligraphy.

"It is a modern piece of work by a local artist. It shows how Allah's path for us is something we can not escape."

Gavin turns to see Dasha standing behind him. He is donning a tux with an undone bowtie slung around his neck. In his right hand, he holds a black case. "That's a bit fatalistic. Isn't it?" Gavin asks.

Dasha looks out across the large rectangular room. "Yes, I personally do not agree with it, but many believe this way. I take it that you also do not agree with it?" he asks, turning to face Gavin. Dasha's expression seems forlorn—weary as if he were a general who had found himself near the middle of an already long, drawn-out war.

Gavin turns back around to examine the tapestry once more, now having gained a bit more knowledge about it. "Even when I was a man of faith, I believed we had some kind of free will. Otherwise you become a robot and lose your explanation for why there is evil in the world."

"You did, however, believe that God was involved in your life?"

"Yes, but the question was always how much." Gavin twists around to look at him.

"Ah, yes, that is the real question," Dasha utters and walks to the seating area that was near the center of the room. He carefully places the black case on the coffee table. He lowers himself down into one of the more comfortable looking seats surrounding the table. He does not say anything but seems to be simply waiting for Gavin's curiosity to take over.

"So that's the job you've been talking about?" Gavin asks while he strolls over to the seating area.

"You will go to the train station in Grozny and purchase a roundtrip ticket for Moscow." He reaches into his pocket and pulls out a billfold. "The Grozny-Moscow line has just been reopened."

"Yeah, I heard that it was destroyed in some kind of terrorist attack, which I'm sure you had nothing to do with."

"As I have said before, we do not participate in such things." Dasha looks down at the case. "At the Mozdok stop, you will open case. A man in red shirt will board the train. The opened case is the way the man will identify you. When he approaches, you will offer him seat next to you. After few moments of polite conversation, you will give him envelope that is inside. You will both continue on to Moscow where he will take you to another man who will give you items for second part of assignment."

"And if I do this, you will let Elizabeth go?"

"No." Dasha peers over in the direction of the marble fireplace adjacent to the seating area. For a moment, he stares into the blackened pit. "This is test. If you complete this test, then you will *see* her."

He places the billfold on top of the case. "Rubles will pay for your roundtrip ticket. You have new passport and new name in the event someone is looking for you. You will tell anyone who asks that you are on your way to Moscow for important meeting because you are assisting with the opening of an orphanage in the republic."

An underling, the height and width of a telephone pole, walks into the room as if on cue, holding a hanger with a modest looking sports jacket and shirt. The floor squeaks with each step he takes in his stocking feet until he reaches the Oriental rug in the center of the room. Gavin wonders how Dasha had entered the room without making a sound.

"We have provided you with new clothes," Dasha explains, gesturing his hand in the direction of the garments.

The underling moves to the other side of the room and pushes on a section of paneling. The segment opens stiffly, revealing a bathroom.

"You may shower and shave. Tomorrow you will board train."

"We had an agreement that you would let Elizabeth go after I did a job for you."

"That is true."

"Are you telling me you are not going to honor our agreement?"

"No, this first assignment is test not job."

Anger begins to stir within Gavin, and even though he was not surprised that a terrorist could also be a liar, he still found himself offended by this abuse of the truth.

"I think I could use you for a great number of things, Gavin."

"I've only offered to be useful for Elizabeth's sake."

"Useful? You are recyclable!"

⚔

In the driver seat of a two-door hatchback, Gavin awakens. Following the refusal concerning Elizabeth, Gavin had lunged at Dasha. After that, he could not remember what happened.

A bit groggy, he peers over to the passenger seat and sees the black case with a map resting on top with a big red X marked on it. Out the front window he sees nothing but land and road. He wonders what they had done to keep him unconscious for so long in order to move him to the middle of nowhere.

Picking up the map, he peels off the note affixed to it and crumbles it in his hand. The poorly written message was unnecessary; he already understood what he had to do, and what would happen if he did not do it.

He bends down, noticing a satchel on the floor. He unzips it. The change of clothes that he had been offered were neatly arranged within the bag. A passport and some other paperwork rested on top. He leans down and bends open the passport. Vincent Keeler was his new name. Immediately taking a dislike to the designation, he tosses the passport back into the bag and glances at the black case.

He had to open the thing, of course, because it was likely that there was no envelope within the case, that the man who was to get on the train to retrieve the thing did not exist, and that when Gavin unlatched the case on the train, it would detonate the bomb within, killing everyone in sight.

Gavin shakes his head. Those comic books from his youth were influencing his mind again. He laughs at his imagination and decides to change his clothes.

CHAPTER 26

After yet another checkpoint, Gavin drives into Grozny. "Good grief," he proclaims at the sight of the war-torn buildings that looked as if someone had run the entire city across a cheese grader. Roofs and the upper floors of buildings had been shot through or completely blown off. *Is this World War II or what?* He is so distracted by the shocking sight that he nearly misses pulling into the train station.

Halfway into a parking space, his car stalls for the third time. The first time it happened, an old man in a rusted out Toyota truck had pulled over and before even stepping from his vehicle had started talking at Gavin in Russian.

"I only speak English," Gavin had said over the man's nonstop chatter, "and maybe a little high school Spanish."

"Ah!" The man had replied. "Let me see what is wrong?" he inquired in English before disappearing behind the raised hood. Gavin knew he was at the stranger's mercy, never having obtained for himself any mechanical skills of his own. His father had been the mechanic in the family and was often found in the garage fixing the cars of his parishioners, while Gavin sat and read books about characters that did things that, up until now, Gavin would have never dared to do.

Feeling the familiarity of waiting for a diagnosis, Gavin had kept himself busy by looking the car over. He kicked at its tires and played with the door handle. He realized for the first time how small the car really was. "It's more like a dot than an automobile," Gavin had said to himself, swiping his hand through his hair as his anxiety surprisingly grew within.

A few minutes later, the man had gently lowered the hood down and then slammed it closed the rest of the way. "You are fixed."

"Thank you," Gavin had said and then offered the man some money.

"No, no," the man had responded, "you will need this. It is good to sacrifice for strangers."

Now, nearly into the parking space, Gavin turns the key of the car a couple more times and then gives up. Exiting it, he moves to the back bumper and pushes the "dot" the rest of the way into the space. "End of sentence," he says to himself with a laugh that mixes with a bad feeling.

Opening the passenger's door of the car, he stands there, leaning on the window frame. With doubts resurfacing again about the contents of the case, he stares at it. In one quick move, he grabs it and slams the door closed.

He purchases the cheapest ticket at the ticket desk, showing his passport. He then notices that he has to go through some kind of security check. This was a good sign. Dasha would certainly have known about the inspection, which from what Gavin could tell looked rather intrusive. And in knowing about it, Dasha would have never bothered to get a bomb through it when all he needed to do was place one on some tracks, and let the train come to it.

He quickly scoots in line behind a woman with two kids. They cling to her skirt and shift forward like one organism. The screener gives them an order. They separate. Each person is patted down. Their luggage is passed over by a metal detector, and they move on, again as a unit.

Gavin gladly places his bag and the black case on the table. He hands the screener with the mustache his passport. The hairy-lipped guard looks at him oddly but then examines the identification. He says something to his partner and slides the case off the table, motioning for Gavin to follow. Gavin turns around to see if maybe the screener was referring to someone else. Seeing no one, he obeys, grabbing his bag.

They enter into a small room with a desk, a chair, and a fan. The screener gestures at the chair. Gavin takes a seat. The screener glances at his watch and lowers the case down beside him. He lights a cigarette.

Perspiration forms on Gavin's brow and beneath his shirt. "What's going on?" he asks.

The screener watches Gavin. He flicks on the fan. It turns and blows, offering Gavin some relief from the stuffiness of the room. It rotates toward the screener. He smoothes his mustache as the fan rotates back at Gavin.

The screener drops his half spent cigarette and smashes it with his foot. "Money for case."

"Ah," Gavin says. His pocket travel guide had warned him about this. It had also offered some advice: *When you encounter a situation where extortion is obviously occurring and there are no weapons involved, hold your ground. Don't give in. In most cases, the individual will give up and seek an easier target.*

Simply curious to see if the advice would work, Gavin refuses. "No, give me back my case."

The man fiddles with his mustache. "Money," he repeats.

"No."

"Money."

"No."

The man scratches at his hairy lip. He waves Gavin from the room, cursing the air with his foreign tongue.

Gavin giggles a little as he snatches the case from the floor. He saunters out the door toward the platform. He turns, hearing a scuffle at the security area. He sees the mustached screener apparently taking his frustrations out on an elderly woman. For all his efforts of intimidation, granny was winning. While enjoying the scene, Gavin's grip loosens on the case's handle as he realizes that the screeners hadn't actually inspected the thing.

Gavin turns his attention to the train pulling up to the platform. Travelers quickly make their way toward it. He peers at the mustached screener and attempts once again to ease his worry with the logic that Dasha would never chance taking a bomb through a security check, but then again...maybe the screener was in on the plan?

Gavin laughs. *No, that would be way too complicated.* Dasha liked to keep things simple. He had basically said so himself.

CHAPTER 27

Gavin boards the train. A female attendant looks over his ticket and then hands it back to him. Any lingering worry that he may have had about a bomb is put on hold when he sees the reality of what a cheap ticket has bought him: absolutely no privacy. The carriage was wide open with rows of bunks and a line of day seats along one wall. *Terrific.*

Taking a seat, he carefully slides the case underneath. As the train jerks forward, the attendant comes around and takes his ticket and a fee for bedding.

As she moves on to the next traveler, Gavin gets the feeling that someone is watching him. He notices a man sitting upright in a cot across the aisle. The man sits with his legs crossed, seemingly only interested in peeling back the next page of his newspaper.

Gavin examines the newspaper closely. He had no need to decipher the foreign headline for the picture revealed all: another attack by Chechen rebels.

Before making the initial overseas trip, he had read numerous articles on the web about the region. From the coverage of the mainstream American media, one could easily get the idea that besides the Moscow theater incident of 2002 there had not been any other terrorist attacks in Russia. The web provided a different story, however—one of ongoing hostilities.

Gavin remembers the description Dasha had given him: recyclable. He imagines himself laying down on a conveyor belt all torn to pieces and then coming out the other end all shiny and new. Why had he given Dasha the benefit of the doubt? Of course there was a bomb in the case.

He glances around again at the other passengers. Why hadn't he just followed through with his earlier suspicions and opened the case back at his car when he was alone? The truth was, he hadn't been ready to go out like that, but now he would have to be ready.

At least, the car was relatively empty. The newspaper man, of course, an old man with possibly his wife, a large sized middle-aged pro-wrestler sort of fellow, and a few groups of women were sitting in the day seats while others had already taken to their bunks.

He wonders what these people had done to have their karma paid back to them in such a brutal way. Possibly, they were all cruel sorts of people who, by their own malicious acts, had brought them to this very car, but this, of course, was far too much like how a stereotypical Christian would view things—or at least how a stereotypical atheist would *think* a Christian would view things. Either way, Gavin, in possibly his last moments of his life, wanted nothing to do with being stereotypical.

His senses heighten. He smells the musky cologne from the lady in front of him. He notices the dense moist air in the carriage and the rock in the pit of his stomach.

In the bunk to his right, he sees the wrestler seemingly trying to put an end to his smoking habit. He throws a cigarette into his mouth but forgoes to light it. He then plucks it from his mouth and exhales into the air. He continues on with this routine as an idea begins to form in Gavin's mind. He could do what Dasha had requested. He could open the case and let the bomb go off but that did not mean that the passengers had to be on board when he did.

Pulling off his jacket, he places it beside him on the vinyl seat. He gestures at the wrestler for a cigarette, and after a few misunderstandings, the wrestler hands him one. Gavin motions for a lighter, and the wrestler obliges with a comment that Gavin does not understand.

After lighting the thing, Gavin coughs a few times and then eases into the habit as he hands the lighter back. The wrestler repeats his previous comment, and Gavin nods his head, still not understanding.

He rests his head back, placing the cigarette next to him on his jacket. He closes his eyes. For effect, he begins to snore softly. He listens to the rumble of the train. The hypnotic rhythm soon becomes the only sound he hears, and his phony snoring is soon replaced by the real thing.

As his slumber deepens, his arm slips off his lap onto his jacket. His arm feels warm—no hot. He awakens fully. His sleeve is lit up like a torch. He bends his arm in front of him unsure of what he is seeing.

The wrestler lets out a girly scream, but he is too early—the flames have not yet advanced. Gavin turns to give the wrestler a disapproving look, but before he can, the wrestler pounces on top of him. Orange and light turn to grey and smoke as the wrestler beats down the flames entirely.

The wrestler is awarded with applause, and Gavin is rewarded with a general sense of inaudible censor. He holds his arm out in front of him. Bits of sleeve flutter to the floor and seat. For the first time, he notices the burns on his skin and then the pain too. He looks around to see if anyone is watching him. Possibly out of disgust, no one seems interested in the dim-witted foreigner. He cradles his arm and waits for the burns to smooth over.

As the fiery sensation diminishes, his thoughts wander to an unexpected destination, to an unlikely future—a future with Elizabeth, where they had a home of their own, children at their feet; dancing in the kitchen, her in his bed. He had once thought this would be his only true outcome, but he had crumbled it up and tossed it away out of fear. He would have to confess, however, that although this destiny had been cut off, she never was. He had kept tabs on her.

There were at least three different ways to get out of his hometown, but he always chose the one that went by her house. A few times he had seen her out in the yard talking to a neighbor or doing some kind of yard work. He was slightly ashamed to admit it, but a couple of times he had eased off the gas to get a closer look at her, but inevitably, there was always a shrub or a neighbor blocking the way.

With his arm restored, he rolls up his burnt sleeve and then the other. He wipes the bits of charred fabric from his lap. He wonders what his future would look like after he set off this bomb. Surely he would not have one. He would not survive it. Or would he? He had only considered this a little; he had not thought it through to any conclusion. He begins to imagine his hands and feet crawling back together again. The idea was ridicules, of course. But what if he did survive the blast? Would he be able to get away? What if he could not and he was caught and accused? Would they put him in some gulag with a science lab somewhere in Siberia? Did they even have gulags anymore?

At that thought, Gavin sees a female attendant pointing in his direction. Acid stirs in Gavin's stomach as he sees a man with an automatic rifle pushing past her. The man advances through the aisle, looking to his left and right, with his face displaying no emotion. He stops in front of Gavin and says something in a low somber tone. Gavin pulls out his passport, guessing at the request. The man examines it. He says something while mimicking the habit of smoking and then points to the area between the cars.

"Yes, of course. Sorry." Gavin says, feigning ignorance.

The man stares at Gavin for a moment. Returning his passport, he walks back the way he came.

Several excruciating hours go by where Gavin spends most of his time in the bathroom, and then the train slows and comes to a stop. Gavin pulls the case out from under his seat. His mind begins to twist and turn. There was no way out of it. If he didn't go through with it, the woman he cared for—no, he had to be honest with himself—the woman he loved would be murdered as the note on the case had indicated. But if he did do this thing, this horrible thing, *he* would be the murderer. But wasn't he a murderer either way?

For the first time in years, despair descends upon him. He is too slow to catch it in its infancy, so it grows until it is an uncontrollable brambling vine, slicing its talons into him and clinging to everything. He beats his fist against his forehead. His brow is covered with droplets of sweat. He wants to throw up.

He waits to see if the car will empty a little, and to his relief, it does. The wrestler and the lady in front of him escape through the door. Minutes from now, they will be glad for their decision.

Adrenaline pumps through Gavin, and he jumps to his feet. He wonders why he hadn't thought of it before. He would simply yell, "Bomb!" and get every-one off, but before he can holler his announcement, he notices someone walking toward him: a man holding a jacket, carrying a small bag and wearing a red shirt. Probably a hoodlum from the day he was born, but to Gavin, he is the most beautiful human being he has ever seen.

Gavin begins to laugh. The laughter is unstoppable, and it rolls through him, displacing the despair that just minutes before had clung to him so tightly.

He fumbles with the case and then places it on top of the seat in front of him. Unclasping the two large metal latches, he opens the lid slowly as doubt continues to intermingle with faith. Then seeing that the man is only a few feet from him, he hoists the lid the rest of the way. Gavin views the contents with satisfying relief. It was just as Dasha had said—a simple white envelope was all that was inside.

The man nods at him and then points to the window seat. Gavin steps out of the way, allowing him access. Before sitting, the man pushes Gavin's singed jacket aside and picks up a couple of pieces of Gavin's burnt shirt sleeve. He draws them close to his oversized eyes that sit precariously inside their sockets. He turns and examines Gavin, sprinkling the pieces to the floor.

The train begins its journey again, and Gavin collapses into his seat. He is physically fatigued. He closes his eyes and has a strange intense desire to thank someone for the way things have turned out. The event has altered him—split his hard outer shell wide open. He attempts to mend it, by reminding himself that there was no one to thank except maybe Dasha or the red-shirted man next to him, who looked more like a mad scientist than a middle man for a terrorist organization, but neither of these men were ever going to get a thank-you note from him.

Gavin reaches into the case to extract the envelope. He hands it to the "scientist".

With his steadfast gaze on the seat in front of him, the scientist accepts the envelope. He then glides it into the pocket of his suit jacket that is on his lap.

Chapter 28

Gavin stares out the window. Field, forest, and, oh yes, surprise, field, and forest once again make up the scenery. From beginning to end, the entire train trip was to take about 43 hours. It would be a long one.

He debates whether or not to converse with the man next to him. He had plenty of questions, but maybe it was best to leave those questions unanswered. He had been saved from a tight spot, and after one last phase of this test, he would be rewarded with seeing Elizabeth. Those were the only parts of this story that he wanted to know about. It was linear and uncomplicated. He wanted to avoid any additional information that could lead him down a path into another nightmare.

Light fades, and the dark conceals the scenery outside. The passengers begin to make up their cots. Gavin does the same in an atmosphere of continuing disapproval. He flops onto the mattress and closes his eyes forgoing to cover himself with a blanket. Hushed conversations continue throughout the car. The words, which have no meaning for him, simply lull him to sleep.

The next morning he awakens and finds the scientist's jacket covering him. Gavin crawls out of bed, taking the garment with him. Finding the scientist sitting in one of the day seats already dressed in another jacket, Gavin hesitates in returning the one he had.

"That's right. That is your jacket now," the scientist informs him while pointing at Gavin's wrinkled and battered shirt, seeming embarrassed by the mess. Gavin shrugs his shoulders and puts the thing on. It was a bit snug, but it would do.

As morning routines give way to a leisurely afternoon where the only things to do are to eat, sleep, and talk, an older man sits down in the day seats across from Gavin and the scientist. Without asking, the scientist begins to interpret for Gavin the traveler's story.

"He is attending funeral."

Gavin nods his head and looks out the window.

"He is retired circus promoter," the scientist continues, seeming undeterred by Gavin's lack of interest. "One of the former performers died, not in the ring but in mundane car accident. This is very bad."

Gavin peers over at the man who is frowning as if he understood the translated words.

The train goes into a turn, and someone, passing by in the aisle, bumps into Gavin's shoulder. He looks up and sees a pretty blond smiling down at him. She says a few words.

"She apologizes," the scientist translates. As she trades a few words with the scientist, the woman slips in beside the circus promoter. After a bit of conversation with the woman, the scientist nudges Gavin. "She is returning to her husband."

"Her husband?"

"Yes."

Gavin looks out the window.

"He had an affair. But now he has asked her to come home. They have come to understand each other. This is very good."

Gavin looks out the window.

The day continues on. The passengers swap stories, travel tips, and food. Gavin looks out the window.

After another night, the train pulls into the Moscow station, Gavin and the scientist remain in their seats as the other passengers exit from the car. The scientist gives each of them a word of farewell. How Gavin had gotten paired with such a socialite, he did not know.

After stepping off the train, Gavin searches for a restroom inside the terminal since the one on the train had been closed for the last hour. When he comes out of the bathroom, the scientist is nowhere in sight.

He is glad for this. After two days of constant human companionship, he needed a moment alone. He breathes in deeply, finding a spot to sit on a bench beside one of the glass enclosed convenience stores that were inside the terminal.

His respite is short-lived, however, by a commotion that seemed to be occurring out of view, around the corner, inside the store. He considers ignoring it, which he could do rather easily with the glass enclosed store being lined with so much product he could hardly see inside, but the sounds of a tussle grow in intensity. Besides he needed a snack.

Leaving his bag and the black case at the bench, he gets up and walks to the door of the store and glances inside, finding to his horror the scientist on the floor. Standing over him is the newspaper reading man from the train. Before Gavin can react, the man pushes past him and takes off toward the front doors of the terminal.

"He's taken envelope," the scientist proclaims opening his suit jacket revealing an empty pocket. He then groans and rubs the side of his head. "This is bad."

"Great," Gavin snaps. This was the kind of path he had wanted to avoid. He runs in the direction of the man which leads him to a parking area out front. He searches the lot and spots the man jumping into the passenger seat of a SUV. *Great, he has an accomplice.*

He notices, to his right, a younger woman sitting in a brand new luxury sedan. She opens the door and begins to get out of the car. "Perfect," he says to himself with a cocky attitude, but knowing full well, he has never stolen a single thing in his entire life.

Disregarding this lack of experience, he moves in behind her. She seems preoccupied with trying to back out of the car without showing too much leg. He taps her shoulder. She turns, making a space between her and the sedan. In one quick movement, Gavin swipes her keys and squeezes into the car. Yelling and screaming, she tugs on his jacket. Paying no attention, he starts the vehicle and pulls away, closing the door as he goes.

Gavin spots the robbers and quickly catches up. There is only one car separating them. He swerves around, causing the tires to screech. Seeming to notice this, the crooks accelerate, making a sharp left turn.

Gavin follows, dabbing the sweat from his brow. He turns up the air conditioning to high.

The man slithers out of the passenger window and fires a few shots. Gavin huddles down. "You are really ticking me off," Gavin yells into the air, but before he can complain further, the crook slips back into the SUV. Gavin wonders why. They then slam on the breaks.

Gavin's body hurls forward as the sedan smashes into the rear bumper of the SUV. A white balloon smacks Gavin in the face. Snow falls all around, but somehow he knows that is not quite right.

A few moments more, and a shadow blocks out the sun to Gavin's left. He turns to see a large figure through the window. Two shots sound, piercing the glass. Gavin feels the instant pressure of a bullet ripping through his chest and the familiar sensation of an intense heat coursing through the middle of his head.

Moments later, he awakens to the sound of his own wheezing. Catching his breath, he sees that the killers' SUV is still in front of him. The familiar sound of an ignition failing to turn over brings a smile to his face.

He jars open the door of the sedan and slowly places a foot on the road. "Surprise, surprise, I'm back alive, fellas" he taunts but then hears the sound of the SUV starting successfully. They pull away leaving behind one broken bumper. *Terrific.*

Gavin pulls his leg back into the sedan, closes the door, as best that he can, and attempts to start the car. To his surprise, it only takes one try, and he is off down the road.

He finds the killers. They are three cars ahead of him, swinging over into the opposing lane, attempting to bypass the vehicle in front of them.

Gavin veers over onto the wide shoulder, overtaking the first car. He hits a pothole, and a piece of the sedan goes off to the right, but then he hears the sound of a collision to his left. He slams on the breaks.

The killers' SUV sits motionless, smashed into the front of another vehicle in the opposing lane. Gavin turns off the engine and throws open the door. He staggers to the killers' SUV and looks into the windshield. Both passenger and driver seem unconscious.

Gavin opens the front passenger door. The killer's body is leaning forward on the dash. Gavin pushes it back against the seat.

He searches pockets. Finding the envelope, he backs out of the car. As he does, something snags his jacket, jerking him back inside. The killer's eyes widen. He releases his hold on Gavin, seeming shocked to see him alive. The killer grabs at a severe wound on his head. For a moment, Gavin has a sense of pity for the man, but then he recalls the shot to the head that he had received by the man's hand. Gavin slips from the car.

Traffic begins to pile up and spectators circle the wreck. He half expects the crowd to gasp at the sight of him, with his bloodied shirt, but he is overlooked for the injured bodies within the two cars. He buttons his jacket, jogs to the car, and drives off.

Dodging the owner of the luxury sedan back at the train terminal, he locates the scientist, who has their bags in hand. He gives him the envelope.

They go out to the street, and finding a bench, Gavin collapses unto it. As he had driven back to the station, he had considered opening the thing. However, it was not until after abandoning the car along the road and holding the envelope within his hand that the temptation to open it had become overwhelming. After a while of walking in the hot sun, however, he no longer cared. His job was to deliver it, not to make a moral judgment about its contents.

The scientist pats him on the shoulder. "This is good."

Gavin nods, stands, and buttons up his jacket again.

After a taxi ride, the duo make their way through the streets of Moscow. Gavin almost wishes he had brought his camera. He knew he would never return.

After a lengthy walk, they head down an alley. The scientist stops in front of a shop with a wood stained door. As they enter, a bell rings overhead. Inside, the store is full of junk. The scientist flips over a price tag dangling from a lamp. "He has nice things."

Gavin scowls at the dusty objects. He covers his nose, disliking the musty smell of the place.

A man shaped like a tractor-trailer steps out from behind a curtain carrying a metal box. Gavin lets out a snicker. If this was a front for a criminal organization, he wondered why they hadn't gone with a more convincing clerk.

The scientist waves Gavin to the counter. The semi opens the metal box, revealing a key and a pistol with wood grips. The scientist pushes the envelope toward the man. The two exchange glances, and the scientist gestures for Gavin to take the contents of the box. He does so, securing them in a pocket inside the black case. The semi speaks, and the scientist interprets. "He says gun is already loaded." The scientist then leads Gavin out the door.

Outside, the scientist looks both ways down the street. He pulls out two photographs from his bag and hands one to Gavin. "This is job."

Gavin examines the print. The picture is of an ordinary house with an impressive gate and fenced in yard, but the picture did nothing to help him understand what the job was. "Do they want me to remodel it or blow it up?" he asks handing the picture back.

The scientist gives him a flat smile. "They want you to kill owner," he explains, offering him the other photo, which is of an older man standing on the sidewalk, seeming unaware that his picture is being taken.

Gavin takes a step back.

The scientist leans into Gavin's space. He skims his finger across the image of the man. "This person has done evil things. He should not be allowed to live."

"Who is this man?"

"He is very bad man."

Gavin looks down the street, feeling a bit frustrated. "What's his name?"

"Officer Nikolai Dzutsev."

Gavin takes another step back. "Listen, I've got no problem killing someone on the battlefield or in self-defense, but to jump out of someone's closet and kill them in cold blood, well that's something entirely different."

"Why would you feel this way?" The scientist watches Gavin with his bulging eyes. "I suspect you thought there was bomb in case," he says, glancing at the case in Gavin's hand, "yet you still carried it onto train."

Gavin grimaces and turns away.

"I would guess that you are kind of man who thinks he has no one to answer to. If I am correct, why would you care about killing a man that you have never talked to, never even met?"

"On the train I did try to…good grief, I'm not a murderer." Gavin swallows hard. "Besides, I could get caught."

"You will not. You will have way in and way out." The scientist points at the black case. "In about an hour, the key can be used to gain access and complete task."

Gavin looks down at the case. "Have you ever completed one of these… tasks?"

"No, I am not murderer."

Chapter 29

Nikolai lived like an emperor. The furniture, the walls, even the TV were trimmed in gold leaf, but upon closer inspection, Gavin can see that it is merely paint. Still, it was all too much, and he gags a little as he moves into the home office.

In the small crowded room, pictures of war hang over busy wallpaper. He steps closer to the one of Abraham Lincoln at a Civil War encampment. He lets out a chuckle. *Man, this guy really likes war.* He half expects the officer to show up in a costume of full military regalia, metals and all.

Moving deeper into the room, he peers out the multi-paned window. Seeing no one in the fenced in yard, he peeks through the slightly ajar door that leads into an adjacent room. Finding no one there either, he takes a seat behind the large desk that fills up a third of the room. Propping up his feet, he leans back into the chair, but he reclines too far and flips back onto the floor. He scolds himself out loud and then hears someone cough.

Peeking over the desk, he sees a man standing near the door, all buttoned up tight in a lightweight grey sweater. Nikolai Dzutsev.

Gavin is slightly disappointed by the everyday attire, but he puts his disappointment aside as he fumbles with the gun. Standing, he is able to get the thing at least pointing in the right direction. "Turn around," Gavin commands surprised by his own words, realizing that this must be the lack of character that Professor Brickley had once spoken of.

Nikolai disobeys, aiming a finger at Gavin. "For this, you will be sorry!"

Awkwardly and with some difficulty, Gavin tries to rack the slide of the gun as he has seen countless times in the movies. "Give me a break," he says under his breath as he attempts it again. "Turn around," he barks at Nikolai, feeling slightly embarrassed by his failed efforts. Finally successful, he orders his command again.

This time, Nikolai complies. "Of all the angles you have not thought," he says as his outrage seems to dissolve.

Gavin knows he should just tell him to shut up, but curiosity gets the better of him. "What are you talking about?"

Nikolai looks back over his shoulder.

Strangely, Gavin only hears a single step behind him before feeling the coolness of an end of a gun at the side of his head. Out of the corner of his eye, he sees a large man beside him. For some reason, the unexpectedness of this flusters Gavin, and before he can fire, the gun is snatched from his hand.

Nikolai is given the weapon. He passes it between his hands and lets out a roaring laugh. "This day, I knew would come." He expresses amusement again. This time, the hilarity ends with a trace of misery.

⅄

Of course, the dining room attempts to look opulent too. Yellow paint drips over the highly ornate moldings and furniture, lending to the room a kind of caramel haze.

Through the dimly lit room, Gavin can see Nikolai and a woman sitting together at the far end of a table. They quietly talk, and Gavin gets the feeling that the guard behind him has made a mistake by shoving him into the wrong room.

As he moves toward the couple, the woman kisses Nikolai's cheek. She then ambles away, disappearing behind a gilded-looking door.

"Please sit," Nikolai requests of Gavin before taking a swallow from the glass of wine in front of him. His thick lips get coated in the stuff, and he pulls a cloth napkin off the table, revealing Gavin's gun beneath. He slides it over to Gavin. "Shoot there," he commands, pointing to a painting on the wall of some 19th century soldier, which was more than likely just a print. "In the heart, hit him." Nikolai pokes at his own chest.

Gavin retrieves the gun from the table and points it at the picture. He then swings it toward Nikolai, aiming it at his head, but the officer's expression does not change. "It isn't loaded, is it?" Gavin guesses.

"No," Nikolai says, placing his napkin over his lap. "It never was, but you did not know this. A professional would have checked. But do not feel too foolish. It would have never fired, even if it were loaded. Broken is the firing pin."

Gavin glances at the big white orchids on the side table. At first glance, he thought them real, but now he could see that they were merely artificial. They were not the only things in the room that were fake.

He rests the gun down, feeling even more ridiculous about thinking that he could have carried out this plan. If there was a purpose to this talent of his, as Professor Brickley believed, it was obvious that it was not to be an assassin.

The realization of this finishes what the incident on the train had begun, which put him in his place, humbled and shattered his arrogance.

These degrading experiences made him feel a kind of homesickness. A homesickness that was not for his town or even for his home but for his routine. He missed the getting up in the morning, working through the day, and coming home again and going to bed. He wished for it, because he knew his role in that routine, and he played it well. He moved through it with confidence and with certainty.

He realizes now that he really was not an atheist as he liked to proclaim. He had a god. And like a god, his routine provided both comfort and security. It even exacted punishment, as it was doing now, if he stepped outside its borders. For this reason, he wanted to go back, forget everything he had seen, and feel its warm embrace. He wondered; however, after everything he had witnessed, if he could really go back and continue in its service.

Nikolai lifts his glass and swirls the drink within. "This gun, obviously it is not yours. Where did you obtain it?"

"A shopkeeper," Gavin mumbles.

Nikolai lets out a baritone groan. "Why someone would send you, an untrained individual with a broken gun, to assassinate me causes me to wonder at your real purpose. I must accept the explanation that the gun was a kind of message, and you were never meant to kill me." Nikolai's eyes seem to beam at this conclusion. He places his drink down and recovers the gun from the table. He holds it in the palm of his beefy hands. "I had my suspicions about who sent you the moment I saw this gun. Favoring this type as he always has," he explains, returning the firearm to the table.

"Placing us on opposing sides was the first war between Russia and Chechnya. Even now, as Russia again becomes a mistress to Communism, I remain loyal to her. Divided and conflicted, however, was the person who sent you. I am partly to blame for this, of course, but so was his mother. When she was still alive she would tell him stories of how her family had been mistreated during another time and another war." Nikolai taps on the gun. "But then, my son, Dasha's allegiance was decided once and for all when his wife—who was a stranger to me—was killed by Russian troops."

"Your son?" Gavin snaps.

The officer nods slightly. "Stories of his exploits, awful tales of vengeance, I have heard. I knew that he was not just doing these things because he hated my country, but because he hated me for being a part of that country. For this reason, hearing of his actions has brought me much pain. I have spent years attempting to track him and his younger brother down in order to bring an end to the revenge that he was hoping to achieve, but he has always eluded me time and time again. And then you come. Out of nowhere you come. I never expected this. I never expected an American. If it is a message that he intended to deliver, it must be a message of reconciliation, but as much as that has brought me peace, the question of why my son would send you still remains."

Nikolai's inquiry was more of a plea than a question, and in Gavin's present state, he could not deny the father of what he wanted most. "He is keeping a friend of mine hostage."

Nikolai's expression sours. He slams his hand on the table and begins to shift away as if Gavin's words have contaminated the space. "You have been put in the middle of this matter, and I am truly sorry for that. My son's reasons for doing it this way does not make sense to me. Why would he not just send one of his own men?"

"He sees me as recyclable," Gavin says faintly.

"What do you say?"

"He sees me as expendable."

"No, I think it is something more." Nikolai stands from the table and walks toward one of the two windows in the room. He pulls aside a curtain panel and looks to the outside. "When you surround yourself with good people, the worst thing you can do is something bad, but when you surround yourself with bad people, the worst thing you can do is something good. Those who would not look too favorably on our reunion, I believe, are the ones my son has entangled himself with. I have a reputation too, you see. There must be no one for him to trust, besides his brother and the shopkeeper who gave you that gun. Under the guise of something criminal, he must have thought that this was the best way to get the message through."

Gavin leans back in his chair. "But why use me? Why not just make a phone call?"

Nikolai steps from the grayish light at the window. "You are right. From what I have considered, it must be worse." Nikolai starts a journey around the table. "Very closely, he must believe that someone is watching him."

"You mean he has a traitor?"

"That is what I think. Attempting to take over his organization, is this person. Who this person is, my son may not even know. How many have joined this revolt, my son may also not know. For this reason, this message that you have brought me must be more than a request for reconciliation. It must be cry for help." Nikolai noticeably swallows, and in returning to the window, he busies himself with pulling the curtains together.

Gavin had to admit that he felt some kindness toward the father despite all that had happened, but suspended above this emotion of sympathy was the thought of Elizabeth. "If you've been tracking Dasha and his…associates, and if this traitor is a part of that group then this traitor must really want you dead. So what do we do when this traitor finds out that you are still alive?"

Nikolai turns slowly. "About this, do not worry." He taps the side of his head. "A solution to this, I have."

CHAPTER 30

The evening's air is close—suffocating. As Gavin walks into the station from the train, he unfasten the second button of the shirt Nikolai had given to him. Who knew Russia could be so humid?

Following close behind is a man with good intentions. Gavin moves slowly in order for this ally to keep up. A heavy set woman, who seems too busy taking inventory of her bags, nearly runs into him. "My knives, my knives," she yells to the short tubby man walking next to her. He gives her a frown and then hurries back toward the train as she places a hand to her back.

Maneuvering around the scene, Gavin quickly finds a spot where he can be seen by both his ally and his enemy. He does not wait long before someone approaches him.

"We have heard that you have been successful. Is this correct?" the man asks without looking directly at him.

"Is Elizabeth all right?"

"Yes."

"Then I have been successful."

The man glares at Gavin and then leads him outside. They end their journey at a parked car where an older man with a sweaty face is positioned in the back seat with his eyes closed. He was either dead from the heat or taking a nap. Gavin could not tell which—either was a possibility.

The young man lifts his shirt up slightly and displays a gun in a side holster.

"You must have heard about me," Gavin offers, "so you know that won't do you any good."

"I know that it will slow you down. Now, you must place hands on trunk."

Gavin follows the order, not wanting to make a scene. The search yields nothing, and the man ushers Gavin into the front passenger seat.

As the trip gets underway, Gavin assures himself that this nightmare would be over soon. Besides, all his ally had to do was tail him and the enemy until they reached their destination and then call for reinforcements. It was a simple plan, but so much rested on it that Gavin's anxiety resurfaces once again. He stomps it down by imagining he and Elizabeth safely at home. Maybe he would ask her out for coffee. Now that would be different, and unlike bungee jumping, that would be a good kind of different.

Gavin rests his head back, feeling the effects of the heat, but before he can close his eyes, he notices the driver repeatedly looking in the rear view mirror. Whatever he was witnessing, it seems to be flustering him. The driver accelerates the car forward, and Gavin turns to him. "What's wrong?"

"Someone is following us."

Gavin's stomach churns. He glances out the back and sees a blue truck tailgating them. Gavin was no expert, but he knew his ally wouldn't be that obvious. He takes a deep breath and watches as the truck turns off onto another street. The man takes one last look in the mirror. "Good," he utters.

Gavin peels his shirt from his sweaty chest. "Does this thing have any air conditioning?"

"Air conditioning is for women—women who wear dresses and do not want their cosmetics messed up."

"Listen," Gavin says, wiping the droplets of sweat that had been trickling down the side of his face, "I've stared down a locomotive, been dropped from bungee cords, and been shot more times than I can count, so if I want a little air in this claustrophobic can on wheels, I will ask for it and not have a single worry about it detracting from my manhood."

"You went bungee jumping? That is crazy," the man says with a kind of boyish innocence.

"Yes, now can I have some air?"

"This car does not have air conditioning, but you can put windows down."

Gavin searches the door for an antiquated knob. "How do I do that in this thing?"

"There is button on door."

Gavin strikes at the switch, and the window slides down, allowing a gush of continuous air into the stuffy interior. "I would have never expected that."

A loud mumble comes from the man in the back.

"I put it on after market? Is that how you say it?"

"Yeah, so you're into soup'n up cars?" Gavin asks, but the man does not answer.

Instead, he pulls a black hood from beside him. "You must put this on."

Without protest, Gavin covers his eyes, and they immediately go into a left turn. He begins to bounce in his seat as if they were on some unpaved road. He searches for the dashboard and grabs tight. "Slow down," he barks, and the man obeys.

It seems like miles before they return to a paved road. Gavin leans back and tries to relax. He had no idea if his ally had been able to follow the diversion off the main road. His only hope was that his ally knew the roads well enough to be able to connect with them later.

Four more turns, in a variety of directions, and the car comes to a complete stop. The engine goes quiet, and Gavin begins to pull the hood off.

"You cannot do that. I will take you in."

⁂

Inside is the familiar smell of mutton and cheap cigarettes. "Let him see," Gavin hears Dasha order. Gavin blinks a few times, trying to adjust to the light. He glances at Dasha who is pointing at the space behind him.

Gavin turns and sees Elizabeth standing before him. His chest tightens at the sight of her, and he has trouble putting together anything intelligible to say. Instead, he studies her—making sure that she is all right. Physically she looked fine—although she still was a bit too thin, but then he notices tears forming in her eyes.

He wonders if those tears were for him, and then a slap hits him across the face, and in case he hadn't gotten the message the first time, she slaps him again, this time harder. Watery eyes meet his, and she is pulled away. "I met the man you shot," she cries. "He was kind to me when he didn't have to be. Did you know that before you murdered him?"

The sting from the slap disappears from Gavin's face, but the blade from her words seeps deeper into another place. Obviously someone had told her what he had supposedly done. He did not deserve a slap for that, although he might deserve it for being willing to do that, but still, he had been willing because of her.

He could not tell her that truth, however. He had to remain silent as Nikolai had instructed. They needed to find out who the traitor was first and how many had joined him. Playing along, he regards her with indifference as she is led into another room.

Dasha steps in front of him. "Women will always expect more from us. It is only natural. They see us as…superheroes. Is that not right, brother?" he asks, placing his hand on the shoulder of the man who had driven Gavin from the station.

"Brother?" Gavin asks.

"Yes, this is my brother. We have nickname for him. Zhyogal. It means, *fox* in our language." Dasha gives Gavin a knowing look and then strolls from the room.

Zhyogal was the traitor. He had to be. If he was not, then Dasha was simply being cruel to his own brother by not telling him that his father was still alive. And what other reason would he have for telling Gavin this bit of information but to confirm that he had discovered that his own brother was the traitor? And that thing about the fox, was that not a clue?

Certainly, Dasha had taken a chance in being so cryptic about his message to his father, but he must have known that the officer would figure it out, but even so, Dasha must have also known that his father, as quick as he was, would have never come to the conclusion that his younger son was attempting to overtake the older.

Zhyogal steps into the space that his sibling had previously occupied. Something seems to have made him jumpy for he glances over his shoulder a couple of times. He then takes a step toward Gavin, "There is one more thing you need to do before we can let you and Elizabeth go."

Gavin slides his hand down the front of his face. He was in need of a shave and a vacation, but this acting gig would have to go on a little longer. "I know this was just a test and that the actual job comes next, but come on, I just murdered someone for you. What more could you possibly want me to do?"

He leans toward Gavin's ear. "I want you to kill my brother."

Chapter 31

Gavin attempts to make the cot beside the kitchen sink as comfortable as possible, but he knew that even after his adjustments it would still be difficult to sleep. He had far too much on his mind—too many secrets taking up residence in his head. The covert rescue mission that was to take place—whenever, Elizabeth's misconception about what he had done, and of course, the secret of his ability, which weaved its way through all of this and would surely have to be explained to her someday. This hidden knowledge mixed together with the worry that the rescue mission would come inconveniently after he was forced to carry out Zhyogal's new request.

And what about Juan? Where had he been all this time? Tangled up in red tape, Gavin supposed, inside some dingy Soviet style cement building where they snickered at his Russian.

The moon shines through the window. The leaky faucet drips randomly. Trying to get these things off his mind, he makes an effort to anticipate when the next drop will fall, but the number of correct guesses begins to wane as his eyelids begin to grow heavy.

A loud bang startles him from his slumber. He attempts to move, thinking that the rescue is in progress, but something is binding his legs together. He cannot see what it is. The kitchen is blacked out; the moon is no longer shining through the window. He gropes in the dark and finds that his blanket has twisted itself around his legs. In vain, he tries to loosen the hold, but he cannot seem to find the end.

He hears a rustling sound at the door and the kitchen light being switched on. Light fills the room, and Gavin shields his eyes with his hand.

"You must get up, and follow me," Zhyogal proclaims, standing at the entrance of the kitchen with a flashlight in hand.

Something like hope drains from Gavin. "Okay, just give me a minute," he grumbles and re-launches his struggle with the bed linen. "I just need to get out of this jam." He lets out a laugh, feeling slightly embarrassed, and then finding the end, he untangles himself from the cover.

He follows Zhyogal across the lawn to the barn. "Take this, and conceal it until it is time," Zhyogal says, exhibiting a handgun.

"When will I know it's time?" Gavin asks, playing along.

Zhyogal does not answer. He slides open the wooden door of the barn. The stench of manure wafts around Gavin, and he turns away in search of a bit of fresh air. He expects to see a horse or a cow inside. Instead, he finds a large table in the middle of the barn with a couple of computers on top.

Dasha is hunched over the table; his attention is on a scrolled out piece of oversized paper. Gavin moves forward and sees that the paper is actually a blueprint for what appears to be a large building.

Dasha looks up from the drawing. He seems concerned as he steps away. His worried look mirrors that of his father's when Gavin had informed the latter that his eldest son had gone into hostage taking.

"What is this?" Gavin asks.

"This is my brother's plan," Dasha explains. "Any questions you may have, you will need to ask him." He then walks away toward the stables.

"My brother does not agree with my plan," Zhyogal interjects, "but it is good plan. Now, we must move quickly." Zhyogal begins to roll up the paper. "We will take you to new location."

"What will you do with Elizabeth?"

"She will not be going to same place," Zhyogal informs him.

Gavin's mind seems to collapses in on itself, but through the narrowing space, there was one message piercing through: He had to do something, and he had to do it now. It did not matter about the upcoming supposed rescue mission. *He* was the rescue mission. He draws the gun and directs it at Zhyogal. Gavin smiles, relishing not only the action that was obviously unexpected but also the clearing away of at least one of his secrets from his overstuffed head.

"Gavin!" Elizabeth shouts from outside. He turns to find two men forcing her in the direction of a car.

"You must aim that at my brother, or those men will kill Elizabeth," Zhyogal clarifies, studying his sibling and wearing the same kind of grin that Gavin had worn just a moment ago.

Dasha's expression, however, does not change. Clearly, he had considered his younger brother capable of murdering him. He presumably was not able to do likewise, and for this reason, the elaborate plan with his father had been set into motion.

Gavin hears what sounds like a spray of bullets hitting the side of the car. The noise of tires popping goes off, and Elizabeth's handlers change direction and race her into the barn.

One of them pushes Elizabeth against the wall, pointing a gun at her. With this leverage, the other removes the weapon from Gavin's hand and closes the barn door. Dasha takes a few steps closer to Gavin.

Zhyogal is handed his gun back. He turns and aims it at his brother seeming to have found the courage that he had lacked yesterday when he had asked Gavin to do the deed. "Who is shooting?" he demands almost pitifully. "Did you plan this, brother?"

"I am saving you from yourself," Dasha answers and then continues in his native tongue. The exchange persists as Dasha exhibits an unexpected calm while rage and tears ring from Zhyogal like water from a sponge as if this rivalry had been drowning him for a very long time. "You have always reigned over me, brother, and I have loved you, but I can no longer follow you."

Gavin, within the confines of his office back home, would have encouraged the younger, obviously stepped upon sibling to continue but here, with guns pointing, encouraging this kind of confession was anything but healthy.

"You've allowed these men to use you," Dasha proclaims to his brother.

"Or perhaps I've used them," Zhyogal counters, moving closer and holding the gun steadily in his hands.

Dasha scowls, "how many have committed this mutiny with you?"

Zhyogal smiles.

"How many!" yells Dasha.

"All of them," Zhyogal answers with a bit of pride.

"I thought as much," Dasha says weakly.

One of the handlers covering the door points his finger up at the ceiling. Gavin seems to be the second one to see it: A circle of flames eating through the roof. Gavin stares at the growing sphere of fire. He is surprised by this medieval method of liberation by his ally, but he decides to use this unlikely approach to his advantage. "Looks like they plan to smoke us out, but it won't take long for this barn to burn to the ground," he utters and then coughs as the smoke begins to descend upon them all.

Somewhere overhead, a large beam splinters and cracks. A loud bang goes off like that of a cannon blast as one of the beams collapses into the stalls behind Zhyogal and Gavin. They both cover their heads as a cloud of ash, smoke and dust encompasses them.

A moment passes, and Zhyogal materializes directly in front of Dasha and Gavin. Zhyogal points his gun at his brother again, and for a moment, a cloud of smoke seems to obscures Zhyogal's view for he frantically attempts to wave it away with his other hand. Dasha takes advantage of this. With the slightest of tugs, he draws Gavin in front of him, as a pop of a gun goes off and a blast of light reflects off the smoke that surrounds them.

Gavin feels the impact of what seems like a red hot poker going through his internal tissue. He crumbles to the ground with his hand grasping his chest. Through the intense pain, he searches for Elizabeth but does not find her for the smoke has enveloped everyone.

CHAPTER 32

Waking, Gavin coughs roughly. He lifts his head and sees a man standing beside Elizabeth in black garb with a kind of breathing apparatus on his back. The man bends down and begins to lift her up. To Gavin's relief, her arms and legs begin to move.

Gavin feels a pull on his arm, and he is hoisted to his feet. He stares into the mask of his rescuer and points back at Elizabeth. The man motions affirmatively.

Outside, at a safe distance, his rescuer lets him go. Gavin's legs tremble, give way, and he falls to the ground. His rescuer strips off his mask. "Are…you… okay?" he asks with broken English while glancing at the bloodstained puncture on Gavin's shirt.

Gavin peers over at Elizabeth who is sitting on the lawn some distance away. "Yes, but I am cold." He rubs his arms with his hands to demonstrate his words.

"Wait." His rescuer trots away to a cluster of vehicles parked near the grove of trees on the driveway.

Gavin continues to breathe in the clean air, enjoying it as if he'd never before noticed the pleasure of this ordinary thing. He watches Elizabeth rubbing at her brow. He does the same and finds a layer of black ash on his hand.

A crash from the barn and the roof caves in. The fire explodes upwards energized by the banquet of wood and debris. It begins to burn steadily, making the scene an hypnotic image, and Gavin begins to understand how, for thousands of years, people were simply satisfied to sit around one for hours.

Behind the barn, the horizon splits into a multitude of layers of orange, red and yellow. The dawn makes the fire less threatening to Elizabeth who looks over at Gavin being cloaked in a blanket.

Loud voices erupt off to her right, and she sees Dasha warmly greeting Nikolai. None of this made any sense. She replays the scene in her mind before the smoke had made it virtually impossible to see anything. She had been watching Zhyogal who had his gun pointed at his brother. She remembers hearing a shot, but Dasha did not fall. Something, no someone had gotten in his way. She looks over at Gavin again. She jumps to her feet and races to him.

A few yards, and she realizes that perhaps the running thing was not such a good idea. She coughs a few times and slows her pace. Reaching Gavin, she collapses beside him. "Are you all right?" she asks as a cough escapes from her lungs.

Gavin draws the blanket closer to himself. "Yes, I'm fine."

"I could have sworn Zhyogal shot you."

"Well, don't be too disappointed. He didn't."

"Are you sure? You're wrapped up like it's winter. You might be in shock."

Gavin wraps the blanket even tighter around himself. "Of course, I'm sure. Besides, what makes you so sure that Zhyogal shot me?"

Something within the barn explodes again, and Gavin moves to shield Elizabeth. He looks at her after the fire quiets, and she gives him a disapproving look.

He backs away and observes the reunion that was going on at a distance. "As you see, I did not murder Nikolai. It was all an act to get Dasha out of the bind that he was in with his brother. In fact, Nikolai is Dasha and Zhyogal's father. And of course, Ovlur is Nikolai's grandchild. Although, I don't think Nikolai even knows that he exists. But I think he'll finally come to know that now." Gavin does not say anything more. He allows those facts to stew in Elizabeth's head.

She straightens herself up and leans toward him, kissing him on the forehead.

"Gee thanks, Elizabeth, but I think I deserve more than just a kiss on the brow. I mean I just protected you from an explosion, was instrumental in rescuing you from a terrorist, and I—"

She softly lays her mouth on his, barely touching his lips at first, but then she seems to lose some control. Gavin is overwhelmed by this, nearly unable to catch his breath, but then she pulls away.

Gavin turns to watch the horizon begin to brighten. "You know, you've been able to forgive Stephen, and probably one day you'll even be able to forgive Dasha, yet you're still not able to forgive me for pushing you out of my life."

Gavin turns to her again and sees the flames reflecting in her eyes as she continues to stare at the fire. She then looks at him as a shadow casts across half her face. "That's just it, Gavin. I could never forgive you for that," she says, allowing a smile to break through.

He begins to say something more but ends short, seeing Juan jogging toward them in a black velour jumpsuit. "Where did you come from?" Gavin shouts as Juan approaches.

"Various root cellars," Juan answers and then pulls something from his pocket. "Here, have a potato."

Gavin catches it and then looks at Elizabeth who is the first to let out a laugh.

"Thanks, guys, I'm glad you find this all so amusing."

"We're sorry, Juan," Elizabeth says, laughing. "It's just the stress. Everything is coming out in odd ways." She stands up and takes hold of his hand.

Turning in the direction of the men whose family drama had entangled her for almost a year of her life, Elizabeth notices a man, emerging from the dimness of the dawn. Dust and ash mask the man's face and clothes. But Elizabeth knows who it is. When she notices a weapon in his hand, she begins to shout a warning. But before the family can react, Zhyogal comes to them.

"Brother?" he questions loudly. "Father?" he says, seeming not to believe that, despite his best efforts, both his father and brother were still alive and well.

Holding out his arms, Nikolai begins to move toward his son, but Zhyogal takes a step back, lifting his gun.

"No!" his father yells, but it is too late, Zhyogal's life is ended with a single bullet.

⚔

A strange atmosphere accompanies the three Americans as they are driven away. For a long time, no one says anything. All seem preoccupied with categorizing and labeling what they have all just witnessed. Then Elizabeth turns from the window. "Do you think," she utters slowly as if it took some great effort to push the silence away, "that sometimes things happen for no reason at all?"

Gavin is amazed by the question. After the horrendous incident that Elizabeth had been through, she still seemed to be wondering if something of eternal value had been achieved among those who had imprisoned her. Of course, Gavin did not see any value in this, but he still wanted to help. "I think everything happens for no other reason than what meaning you subscribe to that happening."

"You would say something like that, wouldn't you." She says, looking away. "But…I was hoping for something more."

Gavin scratches at his head. He knew he could ease some of the doubts that were occurring in her mind. He also knew he had a kind of responsibility to do so. After all, if he still had a job back home, it was his profession to help people.

He looks over at Juan. The doctor was heavily breathing, already sound asleep. *Good.* At least, he wouldn't have an audience. "I failed to tell you something…awhile back," Gavin starts.

Elizabeth seems to observe him for a moment. "What?"

"There was something else that Justin had said to me before he passed away." Gavin lets out a cough to give himself time to arrange his words. "He said that God would continue to walk around the walls that I had built until they crumbled."

Elizabeth appears to think about this for a moment. "And have those walls crumbled?"

Gavin shakes his head. "No, but I have to admit this experience has done its damage."

"Well, don't worry," Elizabeth responds, patting him on the leg. "I'm sure that once you get home you'll have plenty of time to patch them all up again."

Gavin is surprised by the response; Elizabeth's mood was much darker than he had guessed.

CHAPTER 33

Elizabeth is seated across the aisle, one row up from Gavin's seat. She is fast asleep as the plane roars through the sky. Apparently, being a hostage puts an end to travel phobias. Gavin smiles and lets out a long exhale.

The meal cart rumbles down the aisle, and Juan gets chatty.

"Gavin," he says, seeming to want to change the subject from the beauty of Brenda, the flight attendant who has just handed them their plastic trays of food. "There was something I should have told you earlier, but in the midst of all the chaos of trying to get home, I didn't say anything." He peels open the foiled lid of his applesauce.

Gavin does the same, cutting his finger on the edge of the plastic container. He holds it up for Juan to see. "You think I have a lawsuit?"

Juan shakes his head. "In a couple of seconds, you won't have any proof that it ever took place."

Brenda turns around, possibly hearing the lawsuit comment. "Will you need a bandage for that, sir?"

"No, I'm fine." Gavin pulls out the tiny napkin from his plastic utensil bag and wraps it around the cut just for show. Brenda smiles brightly and continues on her way.

"You were saying, Juan?"

"Anyway, when I called my parents at the hotel, I was told that something had happened to Professor Brickley. He's fine now, you understand, but he had a heart attack."

"You're kidding? He didn't mention anything when I called him. When did this happen?"

"They told me that it had occurred on the day you boarded the plane to England."

Another attendant, with a pillow in her arms, stops in front of their seats. She points at Gavin's finger. "Looks like you're really bleeding."

"Oh, yeah," Gavin mopes up the droplet of blood that was tumbling toward his palm.

Juan pulls Gavin's hand toward him. "You're still bleeding." He removes the napkin and looks at his friend.

"I am? I can't be."

"We're going to need some antiseptic and a bandage," Juan tells the attendant who tips her head in puzzlement.

"Excuse me," Gavin shifts his food over to Juan's folding table and slams his own into the seat in front of him. He makes so much ruckus that Elizabeth wakes up.

"Juan," she says and then repeats his name again. Not getting a response, she moves into Gavin's vacated seat. "What's wrong with him?"

"He cut his finger," is all Juan offers.

"He cut his finger? Why did he look so panicky?"

Juan shrugs his shoulders and continues slicing into his triangular piece of chicken with his plastic knife. Elizabeth rolls her eyes and returns to her seat.

⅄

Gavin leans on the bathroom sink and stares into the mirror. He did not look different, did not feel different, but he obviously was different. He examines the cut. Just an ordinary thing to anyone else but to him it was a sign—a sign that he was mortal. Had he started out this way, defenseless to the sharp and pointy things of life? No one, not even his parents, according to Professor Brickley, would have been able to answer that.

But then again, the professor was not right about a lot of things. He had been wrong about that dream of his, hadn't he? Although, he would probably argue that the dream was not about his heart attack but about the actual future event of his death. Whatever the outcome of that would be, one thing was certain—they had not discussed the possibility that his talent might come to an end.

Gavin pats at the cut with a wet napkin and wonders if his ability will switch on again. Somehow, he knew it would not. He looks into the mirror again. He would have to face death someday, and he would probably have to do it alone.

At the thought of this, a kind of loneliness descends upon him as if eternity had unwrapped its arms from about him and let him fall into a dark chasm. A surge of emotion pushes up through his chest, and he begins to weep for his own death. He cries as if he were standing over his own grave.

He realizes that this was the proof that he had been born with his skill, for only once, after Dasha had shot him, had he really considered his own demise. Normal people, on the other hand, must consider this all the time.

So he had never been normal, but now he was. Why now? The question, of course, implied a reason and an intelligence behind that reason, so he throws the question into the garbage can. He wipes his face clean of the breakdown, but the evidence within him remained.

"Were you crying?" Juan asks with a snicker and a mouth full of chicken after Gavin returns to his seat.

Gavin begins to open his meal, "maybe."

With his plastic knife, Juan points at Gavin's chicken, "are you going to eat that?"

"Yes, I'm going to eat that. What is it with everyone being so callous? I come back to my seat obviously upset, and it's like you're not even worried about me."

"What? You think I should be worried that, like everyone else, you'll have to face death someday?"

"Yes, it's very difficult being mortal like the rest of you."

"If you're looking for sympathy from someone, maybe you'll find it from Elizabeth. She was wondering what all the commotion was about."

"Well, there's no longer anything to tell is there?" Gavin picks up the bandage, which the flight attendant had apparently placed on Juan's table. He wraps it around his finger as Elizabeth turns around. He points at it, sours his face and dabs at his eyes as if he were swabbing away his tears. Aggravated, she shakes her head and turns back around.

⬥

The Americans are greeted at the airport by family, friends, and a small group of reporters hoping to capture the return of the weary hostages. The flashes go off, and the cameras catch the moment when Elizabeth is enveloped by her family, becoming once again a daughter and an aunt.

Gavin stands off to the side, unsure about whether or not he wants to be enveloped himself, and then Professor Brickley appears from the crowd and hurries to him. He hugs him tightly and offers an emotional apology.

An invitation to Elizabeth's home circulates through the crowd, and the assembly disperses, leaving Gavin and Professor Brickley alone.

"I no longer have the talent."

Professor Brickley slaps his cell phone closed after a short conversation with someone on the other end. "What?"

"I never thought I'd see you with a cell phone."

"Gavin, what did you say?"

"I am no longer a quick healer." Gavin takes a step back. "And please don't try to test that."

"My boy, I worried as much. When did this happen?"

"I don't know when it happened, but I found out on the plane."

Professor Brickley pauses. "After everything was all said and done," he says to no one in particular.

"Yes," Gavin smiles, "my guess is that my body knew that I was finally safe and that it could turn off its defenses."

Professor Brickley frowns, "Your propensity toward disbelief is downright frustrating," he grumbles and takes hold of Gavin's arm. "Come on, let's get you to the party."

CHAPTER 34

The gathering begins to break up after a few hours, and Gavin finally sees where Professor Brickley has been for the last half hour: in the kitchen, cornered by Thomas. Professor Brickley puts his cell phone to his ear and sits on the couch next to Gavin. He speaks briefly and then hangs up. Gavin begins to say something—a joke about Thomas, but then the cell rings again.

"Well, I've got to go," Professor Brickley explains, clicking the phone closed. "Sheila's coming to pick me up to take me to my meeting." He groans as he stands up from the sofa. "I'll tell you; if I had known God was going to send her my way, I would have never opened my mouth to pray for help with my beverage…problem." He chuckles. "Gavin, I'll see you at our usual spot on Friday."

"Well, I'm not sure if I'll be able…"

The professor gives him a stern look.

"I'll be there."

Professor Brickley nods, heads for the door, and then stops to say something to Elizabeth. He points at Thomas as he does so.

A horn honks, and by the time Gavin gets to the window to try and catch a glimpse of who this Sheila was, her car, with Professor Brickley in it, zooms away.

Gavin waits at the window while Elizabeth says goodbye to the last of her guests. He goes to her after they leave. "You had a peculiar look on your face when Professor Brickley was talking to you. What was he saying?"

"He said that Thomas has an extraordinary gift."

Gavin swallows hard. "What?"

"Yeah, he said that Thomas is quite the prophet."

"Ah," Gavin says, relieved. "Just don't…never mind." Gavin moves out to the porch and then twists around. "You know we should get together sometime…for coffee."

"Oh, you think so?"

"Yeah, after all, Elizabeth, I haven't forgotten about that kiss."

She smiles. "I was suffering from carbon monoxide poisoning."

Gavin rubs at his chin. "I don't think that's entirely true."

"Okay, but it's just coffee. It's not a date or anything."

⅄

When normalcy returns to Elizabeth's life, when doubts are smoothed over by the regularity and expectancy of everyday living, when it is finally accepted that the major events in life sometime happen for no reason at all, a letter arrives in the Kashner's mailbox.

If not for the formal writing and cancelled foreign stamp, the letter would very well have been ignored for days and overlooked by the more critical pieces of mail such as bills and school announcements.

"I've got to go to practice, Aunt Elizabeth!" Thomas shouts from his foothold at the door.

"I'll get it ready for you, just a minute," Elizabeth answers, still holding the envelope in her hand.

"What?" Thomas questions with an irritation usually associated with that of a teenager. He then sets himself on the floor with a huff.

Elizabeth flips the envelope over and begins to tear it open. She unfolds the letter within and begins to read the lines of neat cursive script.

Dear Elizabeth Kashner,

 You do not know who I am, nor do you know the purpose of this letter, but you do know the man who asked me to write this letter. Hopefully by the end of it, if I have done my job well, you will understand its function.

 Dasha Dzutsev was the man who requested this correspondence. I am sorry to tell you that he is no longer living. Even though his father attempted to protect him, he was arrested, assaulted in prison, and then later died of his injuries.

Dasha lived out his life on too many sides, and because of this, he had far too many enemies. Earlier in his life, he acted against the Russian government and supported the Islamists after a family tragedy. But something happened along the way. He began to see these forces as just another authority that demanded obedience. As he started to work against these powers, his life became full of deception to the point where having three captive Americans created the illusion that he was on the Islamist's side.

His younger brother, however, under the growing influence of Wahhabism, came to support the very ideas that his older brother was fighting against. So he needed a way out and forced your fellow American to help him.

But I was not asked to write about this man's questionable tactics. What I was asked to write about was this man's faith. Yes, that is correct, one simple act of love on your part—the attempt to aid his young son—led him to a curiosity. This curiosity as well as a vision sent him to stand just outside your door to listen in on conversations that at first were merely intended to keep you from escaping.

I do not degrade this, since one soul is as important as a thousand, but this could have all ended with just one individual finding salvation, if it were not for this man's willingness to share the Gospel with his stubborn disbelieving cellmate. This cellmate I speak of is I.

Once released from prison, I organized a small church service within my home. We would gather for prayer, Bible study, and a simple meal. At first, I thought the people were only coming for the meal, but after we discontinued it for monetary reasons, the people continued to come. The service has become so full that we have moved into a building in the village and will soon have to consider relocating again since a third of the attendees must stand along the walls to listen to the lessons.

I praise God for this abundance and believe that one of our regular attendees, a young local girl, put it best by quoting a well known phrase that is also found in God's Word, "How beautiful are the feet of those who bring good news." I imagine that by the mysterious unbreakable linking of events and people, surely, Miss Kashner you share in this beauty.

Your brother in Christ,
Gera Petrov

Elizabeth, feeling as if God were sitting right in front of her, lets out a joyful cry. Thomas looks up, runs to his Aunt and gives her a willing hug.

⋏

Professor Brickley reads through the letter as Elizabeth sips at her coffee. He returns it to her and blows his nose with a handkerchief. "It is rare for God to show His hand, and when He does, very seldom do we notice it. You must thank Thomas for insisting that you share the letter with me."

"I will." She casts her gaze to the surface of the table.

"Another refill, hon?" Verda, the owner's wife, asks the professor. He accepts the offer, but their efforts are uncoordinated. While Verda begins to pour, the professor pushes the cup toward her, and the coffee dribbles onto the table.

"Oh my, I am sorry," Professor Brickley says as he goes to wipe up the spill with his napkin.

"Darlin', I'll get that for you," Verda declares, taking the dishtowel from her apron. She then proceeds to dry off the table. "It's been such a long day though, I do appreciate your help," she says, patting him on the shoulder. She then hurries away to another table.

Professor Brickley glances at Elizabeth. "I didn't think I did that much."

"Oh, I don't know," Elizabeth says, smiling, "I'm beginning to think that sometimes the smallest amount of light in the darkest of places can make all the difference."

Professor Brickley pushes his sopping napkin to the side and then looks at her knowingly. "Hmm," he murmurs, leaning back in his seat as if he hadn't expected the comment. He then waves at someone behind her.

"Is Professor Brickley chaperoning our coffee breaks now?" Gavin asks, dropping a newspaper on the table while trying to ignore the article that seemed to be screaming at him: "Local Mayor, Nancy Hartman, Injured in Moving Van Accident."

Professor Brickley retrieves the letter from Elizabeth and slides it in front of Gavin. "You're reading this."

Uninterested in its contents, Gavin ignores the piece of paper and orders a cup of coffee. Professor Brickley pushes the letter closer to him. Out of politeness, Gavin unfolds it and begins to skim the lines.

It is near the middle that he loses some of his composure. He remembers the night of the rescue, the slight tug, which had shielded Dasha from a bullet that surely would have killed him. The letter implied a purpose, a strategy as to why Dasha had not died, and why Gavin's talent had remained in place until that very hour.

"You know Gavin, throughout this whole thing, I've had this nagging feeling that you've been keeping something from me," Elizabeth says as Gavin looks up from the letter. "What is it that you haven't told me?"

Gavin glances at Professor Brickley and then looks at Elizabeth. "I'll tell you someday...when I believe it myself."

ACKNOWLEDGEMENTS

A special thank you to Greg S. Baker for his help with editing and Ana Grigoriu for the design of the book cover.

38178693R00109

Made in the USA
Charleston, SC
30 January 2015